THE
BLENDING
TIME

THE
BLENDING
TIME

MICHAEL KINCH

flux
™

Woodbury, Minnesota

First Edition
First Printing, 2010

Cover design by Kevin R. Brown
Cover images: young man with brown hair © iStockphoto.com/Kevin Russ;
    building/sky © iStockphoto.com/Nikola Mrdalj;
    woman © iStockphoto.com/Juan Estey;
    young man wearing hat © iStockphoto.com/Eileen Hart;
    sky © iStockphoto.com/Ricardo De Mattos

Flux, an imprint of Llewellyn Worldwide Ltd.

Library of Congress Cataloging-in-Publication Data
Kinch, Michael P.
  The blending time / Michael Kinch. — 1st ed.
      p. cm.
  Summary: In the harsh world of 2069, ravaged by plagues and environmental disasters, friends Jaym, Reya, and D'Shay are chosen to help repopulate Africa as their mandatory Global Alliance work, but civil war and mercenaries opposed to the Blending Program separate them and threaten their very lives.
  ISBN 978-0-7387-2067-8
  [1. Science fiction. 2. Violence—Fiction. 3. Survival—Fiction. 4. Friendship—Fiction. 5. Africa—Fiction.] I. Title.
  PZ7.K56532Ble 2010
  [Fic]—dc22
                                            2010024149

Flux
A Division of Llewellyn Worldwide Ltd.
2143 Wooddale Drive
Woodbury, MN 55125-2989
www.fluxnow.com

Printed in the United States of America

To Marjorie,
for her insight, her patience, her love.

CUTOFF

> To All Corridor residents: As of 1 May food allotment coupons will be reduced by 10%. This emergency measure is due to lower-than-expected grain shipments from NorthAm Sector-4. We hope to receive increased shipments from Sector-2 by September.
>
> —*Council vid-memo of 5 Apr 2069*

⌐aym stirred as morning light slanted across his cot. He squinted at the pumpkin sun pushing through layers of smudge. No hint of a sea breeze to clean out the Corridor. He'd need a level-4 breather to hit the pavement today. And now he needed to hit it hard. It was getting too close to Cutoff. When he had turned sixteen, it seemed he'd have forever before sweating about becoming a s'teener. But, bam! Here he was, seventeen and two weeks old—a genuine s'teener, and his angst was gut-churning. Because if he didn't score before Cutoff…

Stop it! There was still time. He could get a real assignment if he pushed hard enough—and, if he got a dose of luck. Today he'd hit the Global Alliance offices. They'd see his potential and wouldn't ship him off to be a dead-man-walking Canal drone.

Jaym tossed off his sweaty sheet and leaned out the open window to stare at his gray-brown world. Every day the same: the tethered security balloon hovering over the hood; whirlwinds of dust and plastic bags dancing in the street below; a few people masked by breathers heading to the metro stairs. Jaym glanced at the slate sky. Typical Corridor summer day. No relief until October, when drizzle would return to dampen his world to a darker gray. Till then it was choking dust, grit, and heat.

As he stretched, the metro vibrated beneath his bare feet. He glanced at the clock. The 0615, right on schedule. If only he could crawl back in bed, pull the sheet over his head and sleep through the day. If only he could forget his approaching Cutoff day. But no. His daysleeper would be here in an hour, so he yanked his sheets and pillow from the sagging mattress, tossed them in his locker, then pulled on shorts and sandals. He sniffed his tee shirt. He laid it on the bed and smoothed the wrinkles with his hand. It'd have to do for today's interviews.

Their unit was stifling, with no relief promised. Still no AC. How many days since the grid went down? Ten? Eleven? Rumor was that Pacific Solar had forty square blocks out. *Infrastructure difficulties* was the usual excuse, yet the Hillside neighborhoods of the Council leaders managed to be lit every night. But here on the flats, no cooked meals, no vid, no lights. There would be an occasional tease of electricity.

Maybe ten minutes of power with neighbors whooping with relief—then, fizzle. Back to the dark ages.

He slammed his locker and headed downstairs.

In the kitchenette his mother stood at the sink in her yellow uniform, slowly stirring her cup of BrekFast. Poor Mom. The grunge assembly-line job required her to wear that annoying yellow outfit. They even made her dye her hair that humiliating mustard yellow to match her assembly uniform—yellow shorts and tee shirt. Even her scuffed shoes were yellow. Only her tee shirt's red and black Tsen-Dow, Ltd. logo broke the total canary look. He noticed dark roots showing in her hair. Should he say something? Her boss could use any excuse to fire one of the line workers. But she probably couldn't afford a new dye kit. Better just keep quiet.

"Morning, Jaym."

"Morning."

Geez, Mom had aged so much these past couple of years. Maybe it was the morning light, but the bags under her eyes seemed darker, cracked with deeper lines.

She glanced up at him. "Why're you looking at me like that?"

He shrugged. "You just look…tired." Not just tired, he thought, worn down to hopelessness. A shadow of his once-smiling mother.

She nodded. "Tired." She looked into her cup. "Yes, I'm tired. Twelve-hour days on the line and I'm pushing forty with no chance of moving up. 'Gotta be young,' says the boss. Says I should be happy to have a steady job, and not heading for the Canal or clearing rubble from Old City." She paused. "What's the point of even going on?"

"Come on, Mom! Remember what Grandma use to say: 'Any day—'"

"Yeah, 'Any day above ground is a good day.' Well, Grandma's not having any good days now, is she?"

Jaym bit his lip. Her bitterness and despair had grown deeper each day. And maybe it was catching. There had been three suicides in their building this year alone. He cleared his throat. Had to change the subject. "When's washday? My tee shirts are—"

"Not for a week, but today's a dampday."

"How much?"

"Four liters. Do a tee shirt or two, but don't even think about a shower or washing your hair."

Good. Better her predictable lectures than her whirl-pool of hopelessness.

"But I really need a shower. I've got interviews all week."

It had been seven weeks since he'd finished Tech School. Most days he stood in lines, filling out applications, smiling into interview cameras at placement centers. So far, *nada*. But he told his mom he had possible second interviews with a couple of places. Anything to give her some hope.

She finger-pressed his cowlick. "Use a little gel and your hair'll look fine." He saw a hint of softness in her eyes as she patted his hair. She looked him up and down. "You look pale, Jaym. You feel okay, Honey?"

He shrugged and forced a grin. "Come on, Mom. I

was *born* pale. Thank Grandma Johansen for my corpselike complexion and eyes."

Mom put her fists on her hips. "Cut that out! You're a good-looking boy."

Jaym opened his mouth.

"No! You run yourself down too much. You've got a nice face with beautiful hazel-green eyes. And your freckles—well, they're just freckles. Nothing wrong with freckles." She poked his biceps and shook her head. "You're losing weight, Jaym. You've got to eat more."

"More of what? We're down to one ration coupon and it's a week till issue time."

"It's not like we have nothing. Maybe nothing to suit your gourmet palate, but we have basics to get us by." She looked at her watch. "We'd better get going. Be sure to eat something before you leave."

"Any leftovers?"

She shook her head. "And we're out of cereal till ration day."

Jaym shrugged. "I'll grab a ProtBar." He leaned against the sink counter and unwrapped a bar. Although it tasted like sawdust and ChemSweet, the bars were cheap. Ten bars per coupon.

As he chewed, he read the fine print on the wrapper. *Proudly made in South Corridor by RefuCorp, a non-profit organization.* It should read, *Made by the sweat of refugee slave labor.* Most people knew the Council Director owned RefuCorp. Non-profit? Yeah, for the camp 'gees. But how come the Council Head's mansion looked like a hilltop castle? Word was that kickbacks from the ProtBar operation were spread around the Council, and even up the ladder to honchos at Global Alliance Headquarters. Somehow nothing trickled down to the flatlanders. Oh, that's right! The wrapper says non-profit.

A bass thumped from the Chavez-Smith side of their apartment. His mother shook her head. "That's so foolish. They'll run through their reserves, then what? They'll have nothing."

"Can't we tap our backup just a little?" he asked. "How 'bout an hour of vid tonight. I'm going nuts without—"

Her face darkened as she waved him quiet. "No. I am *not* like your spend-it-while-ya-got-it father."

The dad-lecture. Was Dad even alive? It'd been three years now. They probably grabbed him for Canal work. Last time he saw Dad was after he'd lost two months of coupons in Vidpoker. When Mom found out she screamed and tried to hit him. He held her wrists until she dropped to the floor sobbing. She said she couldn't live like this anymore—that she was leaving. Later that night Dad came into Jaym's room and knuckle-rubbed his head. Said not to be scared, that things would be all right. He'd be on his feet in no time. On his way to school the next morning, Jaym glanced back to see Dad watching from the window.

Dad never even left a note.

His mother now stared at Jaym. He knew what she was going to say.

"Where are you trying today?"

He wadded his bar wrapper and looked down at the scuffed linoleum. "C.G. Row."

"Maybe you should try something more realistic, Hon. You've got to *know* somebody in Corridor Government to get a job."

"Gov jobs aren't impossible. Jos Susnec walked into Corridor Enforcement and got a patrol job on the spot. Two openings happened while he interviewed."

Her back stiffened. "That's because cops die. Especially around here. I *won't* let you die."

"I'm *not* talking about being a cop. But it's possible I could walk into a gov office right when they have a hydro opening."

His mother sighed. "Jaym, there are too many hydro techs out there. I wish you'd gone into solar."

He flushed. "You know I worked my butt off just to pass radiation dynamics! The Hill kids hire tutors to get through. Or they bribe a grading assistant. I didn't stand a chance!"

"Okay, okay." She emptied her cup then grabbed her sack lunch and yellow breather. "Jaym, please just find something before they put you on the Canal or in the infantry." She looked aside, chin trembling. "I couldn't stand it."

He forced a smile. "I'm gonna get lucky today."

"Yes, lucky," she mumbled. "Just remember there're only—"

"Five weeks till Cutoff. I *know*, Mom!" He turned from his mother to towel ProtBar oil from his fingers. Five weeks.

If he didn't get placed, he might risk flight to another sector. He had considered running north, but the CanAm border was tight. Even if he made it across, he'd probably end up in their 'gee camp. Or worse, deported back and sent south for Canal Duty.

His mother wiped tear-smeared mascara. "What about a clerical or supply job in the military? Your tech scores would keep you out of the infantry."

"I'm gonna keep trying for hydro. I'm good." Not great, he thought, but good enough—if he could catch a break. Just one freaking break.

She nodded. "Okay, hydro. Good luck, Hon. See you at 1800."

"Just a sec, Mom. Your hair's messed up here." He fluffed brittle yellow strands, trying to cover gray-brown roots.

She gave him a quick, tight hug then hurried out the door.

He dropped his wrapper down the 'cycler and drank a cup of tap water the color of weak tea. As he sipped he thought about his default choices. Yes, there was always military service, a step above Canal duty. Military pay was near zero, but you had your own bunk, unshared by daysleepers. Rumors were that infantry had a one-in-four chance of getting killed or maimed, but he'd scored high in the Corridor Placements so they'd probably put him in an office or on tech surveillance. Maybe even quiet border duty. But if they assigned him to a hot spot—say a riot or rebellion—they'd grab anybody in uniform to engage in firefights and kick in doors.

Enough of that. Had to be positive today. Needed to impress the Corridor Government interviewers. He grabbed his breather and daypack, then checked the street. Looked safe. Just a few kids on their way to school. He bolted the steel door and headed for the metro entrance.

He made it two blocks before he heard a sultry voice. "Hey, Jaym, remember me?" He glanced at the wall vid and stepped aside the increasing foot traffic. He sure did remember the babe in shorts, tight tee shirt, and hardhat. Gov propaganda of course, but she was always worth a look. He'd never admit it, but her eye contact and calling him by name helped relieve his loneliness. Too bad she wasn't interactive, but still, she said his name, and she'd always be here.

The vid girl smiled as she climbed down from a spotless digger. "Glad you stopped again, Jaym," she said in her silky voice. "Join me, Jaym. Be a part of history and help complete the Canal. All you have to do is drop by your local Canal recruiter." She winked and flexed a tanned biceps. "I've never been so fit and proud of what I'm a part of. Together we can bring MexiCal back to life. Refugees will resettle and replant orchards. So please—"

He walked on. Was anyone desperate enough to fall for Canal recruitment? Sure, his vid babe had her shiny new digger and a perfect bod, but everyone knew Canal work was backbreaking, and deadly. Rumors were that one or two thousand had been killed this past year. Cave-ins, rock falls, idiots at the controls of monster diggers who were forced to make their distance quotas. Were those quotas measured by dead s'teeners per day?

Jaym crammed into a metro carriage and held on as it accelerated. He noticed a couple 'tooed guys sizing him up. He elbowed through the crowd to the next car. There he shared a chrome pole with a girl about his age. Her designer breather—this year's model by Hil Martien—perfectly matched her tan. Embossed mask-lips curved in the hint of a smile. She had to be from Kirkwood or Edmonds Sector to afford that mask. Her icy blues stared beyond him.

He leaned with the packed crowd as the metro hissed around a bend and braked into Sweethome Station—his stop. No words, just grunts and the shuffle of feet as two dozen passengers jostled out with him. Weird how you could shuffle with the other lemmings yet be totally alone—ignored. Did others feel that way? Though it's not like you could ask—*'Scuse me, ma'am or sir—Do you ever feel alone—even lonely—in this swarm of people going to where the hell ever they're going? Pardon me, Miss, but have you ever felt like hanging yourself like my neighbors?*

By the time Jaym walked the six blocks from the metro station to Government Row, burning tears streaked his cheeks. He should've grabbed his goggles. The heat, dust, and smog had settled thick in this sector.

The address he had for the Gov Placement Center led him to an ancient cut-stone building crowded by towering concrete units. Before he pushed through the glass doors he wiped the sting from his eyes. Once inside, he slipped his breather in his back pocket and smoothed his hair.

In the immense entranceway he gawked at the ceiling soaring above pink granite pillars. Couldn't be real granite—had to be painted concrete. He fingernailed the nearest pillar. Damn. The real thing, with different-colored crystals and tiny fossil shells. Perfectly cut and polished. He'd heard all these fancy old buildings had been torn down and the pieces divvied up for the councilors and other wealthy collectors on the Hill. Ornamental buildings were wasted resources, proclaimed the Council. Yet this one stood. Maybe it once was an old church attended by someone with connections. Hard to tell what it had been since this level was now remodeled into no-nonsense office complexes with a maze of hallways.

His footsteps echoed as he approached the information desk. The elderly woman at the counter didn't even look up from her vid pad as she spoke in a robotic voice. "Welcome to the Global Alliance Placement Center. First-time, or repeat applicant?"

"Alliance? But, I thought this was local Corridor placement."

She glanced at his face, then his wrinkled tee shirt, and frowned. "The Corridor Government offices relocated to Seattle Sector last year."

He winced. "But that's clear across the Sprawl."

"The Corridor Complex," she corrected, her tone brittle.

"Sorry—Corridor." Damn, he thought. It'd take most

of the day to make transfers over there—even if he had enough metro passes. "Okay, Alliance jobs here. Does the Alliance ever have hydro openings?"

The woman hesitated, then lifted a brow. "You'll have to ask at *Applications*. Fourth door down the hall to the right." She dismissed him with a flip of her hand.

He found the door and read the stenciled words:

GLOBAL ALLIANCE
NORTH AMERICAN SECTOR
APPLICATION CENTER

Should he knock? No, this was an application office. He took a breath, straightened his shoulders, and stepped inside.

Oh crap. At least twenty others ahead of him, all crammed on benches. The stifling room reeked of B.O. mixed with a confusion of perfume and aftershave. He tore ticket number "0113" from the autoteller. Up front the two interviewers worked behind glassed-in offices. 0082 glowed above one door, 0083 above the other. And his was 0113? Damn.

By 1400 his stomach rumbled. At this point even a ProtBar would be good. At least the numbers above the door now read 0110 and 0111. He turned his ticket over and over.

A heavy-set man with a sheet of paper came out of one office. Number 0112 flashed. Jaym looked around the room, but no one stood. Twenty seconds, thirty seconds…

0112 morphed into 0113. He stood, squared his shoulders and walked toward the interviewer.

Inside the cramped office the girl waved him to sit. "Almost finished," she said, wanding a vidpen at the screen. She looked no more than twenty. Bronzed hair cut neat and short. Her perfume filled the space with tropical flowers. *Plumeria*, if he correctly recalled the scent from a street vid.

"Okay, scan, please."

He palmed the scanpad. She stretched and cricked her neck. "It's not reading. Wipe your hand and re-scan." He rubbed his palm on his shorts and tried again.

"Much better." Data streamed across her screen. "Surname and given name."

"Jaym ... sorry, Johansen," he said. "With an 'e.' Given name, Jaym."

"Chin on the pad."

He leaned forward. Amber beams swept his irises.

"Done," she said. She tapped the screen. "I'm doing the data cross."

He cleared his throat. "I'm probably data-tagged for hydro, but I did well in solar. I'm motivated to be an asset to any solar program."

Contact-green eyes glinted at him—hint of a smirk. "The data match won't allow it. Your solar score is eleven points beneath cutoff. Not bad, but not good enough for the wait list. And your references are weak. No Council connections either."

He felt as if he were sinking, slipping underwater.

The woman leaned back, tapped apple-green nails on

her desktop. "Well, Jaym Johansen with an 'e,' I see you're getting close to Cutoff."

Was she reconsidering? Had to keep his shoulders square. Make confident eye contact.

"I assume you know your options. Have you seriously considered the military? Volunteers have more choices than draftees. Certainly better than Canal duty. In the military there are many opportunities for vocational—"

He worked to keep his voice steady. "No, please. I—I must be qualified for something else."

She fingered a jade earring and looked back at the screen. "Okay, your interpersonal tests are promising. Hmm. Good marks in cross-cultural. And you've volunteered at the refugee camp. Commendable."

He didn't tell her that he'd been assigned to brush clearing around the camp perimeter. And he only did that to get out of hand-to-hand combat class. Never set foot inside or saw dusties up close. If she dug deeper in his file he'd be a Canal rat for certain.

She pursed her lips. "Ever heard of the SUN Colonist Program?"

"Sun? That have something to do with solar tech?"

"No. It's 'S-U-N', all caps. Stands for 'Society to Unify Nationalities.'"

"Like the old United Nations?" asked Jaym.

"No. The Global Alliance replaced the U.N. concept, but with a much stronger hand to enforce peace."

More like a stronger fist, thought Jaym.

"SUN hopes to break down the tribal and racial barriers that have plagued the planet since we came out of our caves."

"Good luck with that," said Jaym.

The girl pinched her lips. "Do you want a chance, or just make sarcastic comments?"

Jaym sat straighter and cleared his throat. "No, ma'am. It's just that since I've never heard of SUN and, um ..." He coughed. "Sorry."

She leaned back, eyeing him. "SUN was founded by a colony of Dutch Quakers, not long after the sea swallowed the Low Countries. The movement does not push religion. The Quakers have been quietly working with volunteers and charities for years, trying to help heal those areas ravaged by war, drought, and disease. But, as you know, most charities are now as withered as MexiCal. The Global Alliance, however, has given SUN a grant of seed money to launch SUN's Colonist concept. At this point it's experimental, but if the program succeeds it could resolve several global ... issues."

"SUN Colonist," said Jaym as he rubbed knuckles on his thighs. "I'd be a SUN colonist—somewhere?"

"Africa."

He opened, then closed his mouth.

"Is Africa a problem for you?"

"It's just that ... Africa is toast. AIDS-III, the wars, the Great Flare. I heard the Flare alone killed millions."

"Yes, Africa has been through all of that, but people have survived. They desperately need ... help. Although it's a trial program, the SUN concept may be their salvation."

Jaym chewed his lip as he thought. *Would he ever see NorthAm again if he was sent to Africa? And what about Mom? At least she might get some Alliance comp money to make up for the little he brought in. He knew families of kids sent to the Canal who got extra rations. At least that's what an Alliance DocuVid claimed. And Africa couldn't be as bad as going to the Canal. Nobody comes back from Canal work.*

He took a long breath. "I suppose there's still fighting in Africa."

"There are Renegades, but the Alliance is providing adequate troops to protect Colonists." She glanced at the clock. "You're over our allotted time. 'Yes' or 'no' to Colony Service?"

"But will I—"

"*Yes or no!*"

'GEE CAMP

"No hay mal que por bien no venga."
(There is no bad that comes without a good.)

—*MexiCal proverb*

———————————

The refugee camp sprawled to the northeast, across the desolate flats of the Corridor. Behind the camp's endless fence, Reya Delacruz walked hand-in-hand with her little sister. Leeta's small hand was warm and moist in hers. Each girl carried a plastic bucket as they headed toward the water truck for their daily ration.

This was the monthly Coupon Day—a day Reya hated. But she couldn't let Leeta see her anger. Had to put on this monthly act and stall for at least an hour before heading back to their tent. Reya detoured Leeta around faded tents rustling and flapping in the constant wind.

She told Leeta these detours were a game, a way to make fetching water more fun. But making anything 'fun' in 'gee camp was all but impossible, especially today. It hurt so much to see that young gleam of hope in Leeta's eyes fade during these last months of heat, hunger, and monotony.

Today most inmates hid in the shade of their tents. Others paced the fence for exercise, or stood in the baking sun with the hundred others lined up at the commissary. Nearby, under a large open tent, Mrs. Guzmán worked with the younger orphans, holding up pieces of cardboard with one-syllable words. The children chanted: "DOG! CAT! RAT!" Reya smiled. Thank God there were a few women like her. Those kids hardly stand a chance, but Mrs. Guzmán gives them a glint of hope and purpose. You'd think the Corridor government would set up some sort of school in this hellhole. After all, a few kids might get a Corridor placement. They'd be shit jobs, of course, but better than rotting here or being shipped to the Canal.

Reya leaned down to check Leeta's breather. 'Gee camp didn't get much Corridor smog, but winds whipping across the flats brought grit and choking dust devils. She stroked Leeta's hot cheek and adjusted the mask. "That better?"

Leeta nodded.

Reya steered Leeta upwind of Latrine Alley to avoid the stench and clouds of flies. As in each day's walk, they paused at the section of the fence where the wind sang through wire mesh like a chorus of spirit voices. Some evenings, when the sun dropped low and the wire was cool enough to touch, Reya would come out to press her palms to the mesh and shiver at the harmonics vibrating through her hands. She thought of it as a harp, a way to recall the music she and the other 'gees left behind in MexiCal.

A hundred meters beyond the fence a Trans-Corridor

metro streaked past. A blur of faces stared at them as the Corridor-born sped past to their real lives.

"Wave at the train, Leeta." The little girl squinted into the wind and waved at the passing train. Reya took her hand and they walked on.

Dust rats, the guards called Reya and the other 'gees. "Dusties" if they were in a lighter mood. But during camp inspections by Corridor officials, the guards were careful to say, "Refugees." When Alliance overseers made their annual visit, Reya and her fellow 'gees enjoyed seeing the Corridor guards and officers strut like tin soldiers and kiss Alliance ass.

"Okay, Leeta," said Reya. "Now you choose the way."

"I just wanna get the water and go back. I'm hungry."

"Sure, Hon … in a few minutes. Hey, wanna check out the new arrivals?" Leeta swung her empty bucket and shrugged.

"Okay, Sweetie. Just don't stare. Remember how people stared when we arrived? We don't want to be rude like that."

"I'll just look a little," said Leeta in her grownup voice. Reya squeezed her hand as they walked past the Arrivals area.

The Arrivals baked under open tarps. Reya noticed the numb stares of six ribby children following the two girls. If they were lucky, the kids would get meal rations soon, and a real tent—in a few days, or weeks.

She remembered how her mom tried to make their hot, wind-flapping tent into a home. Theirs had been little more than four canvas walls with a tarp roof, plus cots to keep them above the dirt floor and the evening skitter of roaches and mice. Mom had hung the old family crucifix from a tent pole, then spent days digging through trashcans for clothing scraps. She tore the scraps into strips and for weeks wove them into a soft, raggedy rug to cover much of their dirt floor.

Although camp life was a dusty hell of boredom, hunger, theft—and occasional violence—at least there were no dunes. Leeta had another nightmare of the old place last night. Dunemares, she called them. So many nights she'd wake up sobbing, gasping for breath. Mom would hold her, rock her in her arms. "It's okay, Hon. It's okay. No dunes. No more dunes. We're far, far north of them. They can't get us."

Reya had similar dreams, but they were faded now. In her worse dreams the dunes oozed toward their old house like brown amoebas. Dune fingers crept across the withered corn patch, smothered Mom's struggling zinnias, and silently flowed around the house to rise above windows and doors as they slept.

Reya snapped from her thoughts when Leeta asked, "Why does Mom want us gone when Remington comes?"

She smoothed a lock of Leeta's black hair, avoiding her large, questioning eyes. "It's just that ... Mom needs extra time to get our ration coupons. They have to ... talk about it so she gets the right amount." *God, could she know?* But Leeta said nothing, just swung her pail as they walked on.

Refugees got a meager ration of food, but for toothpaste, soap, or any other "luxuries," as the guards called them, you needed coupons. Anyone in camp who could walk had to pull shifts in the camp's ProtCorp assembly lines to earn coupons. The guards, however, would trade coupons to 'gees for jewelry or certain "favors."

Mom's wedding ring went first, and then the silver cross she had always worn. But to Reya the greatest loss was Grandma's old mantle clock. Even though the glass face had broken on the journey north, its tick-tocking always brought back the memory of Grandma's house, the sparkle in her coal-black eyes, and even the ever-present scent of her cilantro-mint salsa. Outside Grandma's house grew an ancient oak tree that Reya climbed nimbly as a squirrel. From her highest perch she could see beyond vast orchards to mountains hazy in the distance. She loved the vast open spaces of that land, spaces that allowed her to dream she could walk to those mountains, or even the ocean beyond.

Back then the dunes were only a dark tale told by families fleeing from the south in wagons or on foot. But Reya knew something that far away could never touch their vast valley or Grandma's ranch house. She would always be free to chase rabbits through fields or collect a basket of acorns in the shade of the great oak.

———————

A month after the clock was bartered for coupons, Mom finally gave in. Reya remembered when she saw Remington leaving their tent. He had stepped out buttoning his shirt. He didn't see Reya, so he whistled as he sauntered back to the guard's compound.

Reya had burst into the tent. "*No*, Mom! Why?! Please tell me you didn't!"

Mom wiped her eyes. She knotted her fingers and looked away.

Reya screamed and threw the lantern across the tent.

Mom's face had flushed, but she lifted her chin and snapped back, "I had *no choice!* He threatened to cut our rations in half. I'm *not* going to watch you girls go hungry!"

"I'll report him to the Commandant! Don't *ever* let the bastard—"

She grabbed Reya's arm. "Stop it! Remember what they did to Maria Sabiná when she reported a guard? The burns? Her broken teeth?"

The rest of that night had been a blur for Reya. She did remember the numbing pain of beating her fists against the wire mesh and screaming like a wildcat. Guard-tower spotlights had quickly beamed on her, but after a few moments, moved away. Just another dustie who'd lost it and was pounding her knuckles to the bone.

———

The girls finally filled their pails and started back. It had been an hour. Surely enough time.

"Hey, *chicas*," came a leering voice from a tent shadow.

Reya glared at the scrawny boy stepping into the sun-light. "Beat it, Lobo." She pulled Leeta closer.

"You're a s'teener now, Big Reya. Saw it on the board last week."

She hadn't told Leeta the she'd turned seventeen—a s'teener. The age for service. 'Gee s'teeners were ripe for Canal duty or the infantry. She could be assigned within the month.

Lobo crossed his arms and grinned. "When you leave, who's gonna watch out for li'l sis?"

Reya fought to keep her voice calm. "Leeta, go to the fence. I need to talk to Lobo for a minute."

Leeta stared up at her, wide-eyed.

"Go on, Hon. Hey, I hear another metro coming. Wave at the people for me. I'll be right there." Leeta looked over her shoulder as she shuffled away.

Reya set her bucket down and walked toward Lobo. The boy's grin faded and he took a step back.

"You goddamn better leave Leeta alone. If you even talk to her—"

Lobo held his palms out. "Hey, easy, chica. I'm try-ing to do you both a favor. Los Lobos will protect her. If not my gang, another will get her. You think your Mom'll watch out for her? Hell, she'll probably teach Leeta to—"

Reya put her weight into a punt to Lobo's crotch. He folded, gasping in the dirt. He tried to crab away from her. She stepped on his back and hissed, "If you *ever* try to recruit her, I've got friends who will dangle your little *cojones* from the razor wire. Got it?"

Lobo vomited.

Reya found Leeta by the fence. "Did you wave?"

Leeta nodded, her eyes anxious.

"It's okay, Sweetie. Don't ever talk to Lobo, okay? He's a bad boy. I promise he won't ever hurt you, but you have to stay away from him. Okay?"

Leeta nodded.

They walked on with their buckets. "Reya, when are you leaving me?"

Reya shuddered, but forced a laugh. "Hey, do I look like I'm leaving?"

Leeta kicked a rock with her tattered sandal. "Some of the girls say you're gonna leave 'cause you're a Teener."

"Yes, I'm now a s'teener, but sometimes it takes months—many months before s'teeners get their assignments."

"But, then you'll leave us, right?"

"Hey! We're back home already." *Damn, the tent flap is still closed.* "Hey, Leeta, we forgot to check the bulletin board. Mom likes to know about any camp news."

"It's too hot."

Reya steered her away. "Come on, Sweetie, it'll just take a minute."

They set their buckets in the shade and walked back to the camp bulletin board. In the midst of sun-faded slogans—A CLEAN CAMP IS A HEALTHY COMMUNITY and CRIME REFLECTS ON ALL CAMP RESIDENTS—was the list of incoming dusties as well as the printout of assignees. Eleven outgoing listed today, but she rarely saw anyone she—

She clasped hands to her mouth. "Oh my God," she whispered. "Already."

She read her name again.

CHOICES

To: D'Shay L. Green
From: Asst. Placement Secretary
Re: Greetings

Congratulations on turning age 17. You are now ready for placement by the Council government. As you are aware, the Council will balance what is best for the Global Alliance, the Corridor Region, and, of course, your request for placement. Therefore report to Region Corridor Office #117 in Monroe Sector, Monday the next (5/17/69) at 0915 sharp. At that time you will receive your placement order.

cc: Sector chief; Sector P.D.; Global Alliance Hdqrs.

———————

'Shay glanced at the address penned across his palm. He edged down the dark sidewalk checking numbers on rusting doors.

A HeliCop with its sweeping searchlight swooped overhead. He ducked into a doorway shadow. Damn, he thought, shouldn't be so jumpy. He hadn't done anything wrong, but with his skin tone, it wasn't healthy to be in this hood. Anybody asks, he got lost looking for his Uncle Twizz somewhere here in WestBay Sector.

He scanned the street. Few signs of White Pride in this Caucasian neighborhood. Not unless you appreciated sidewalk drunks, stripped cars, and brainless graffiti. This made his hood look upscale.

He walked on and found a faded 1371 beside a door. He squinted at the names scrawled beside the buzzers and pressed one. Half a minute passed before an annoyed voice crackled through the speaker. "Yeah?"

D'Shay recited: "A good night for a walk."

A pause, then the voice said, "No chance of rain, they say."

"I heard it was 10 percent."

"Okay, who sent you?"

"Hatch LaBarre."

"Level-16. 'Harrison' on the door." The lock clacked open and D'Shay stepped into a hallway that reeked of moldy carpet, cat piss, and cigarettes.

The shaky elevator rattled slowly to Level-16. He found the door stenciled "L. D. Harrison, Ltd." He rapped five quick knocks.

A metal visor slid open to show a bloodshot, pale blue eye. The visor slammed and the door opened. "Inside, quick," said an egg-shaped white guy. Humpty Dumpty's head was shaved—a little dented on the left side—and he'd sprouted a patchy red beard. He had pouched eyes and wore a half grin, like he was on junk. This was the guy who was supposed to save him?

He crunched through peanut shells littering the threadbare carpet. Humpty deftly cracked a handful of nuts, letting shells drift to his feet. He chewed peanuts and waited for D'Shay to speak.

"I need a different s'teener assignment. LaBarre said you were the best."

The man leered. "I *am* the best. So, what'd you get? Canal duty?"

"Yep."

"LaBarre couldn't set you up?"

D'Shay shook his head. "Said I'm too mucked up for him to help."

"Great. So, what are we up against?"

"I been fostered out six times; in the Youth Pit six months for lifting merchandise—mostly groceries; kicked out of school for—"

"Enough," said Humpty. "Yeah, you're out of LaBarre's league. Good he sent you here. You bring cash?"

"Got it."

"Well, let's see what we can do." Humpty plopped before his vidcom. "Gimme a palm."

D'Shay laid his hand on the pad. The screen came alive with multi-dimensional layers of data. "Show three, six, and eleven," the man told the screen. Layers shifted. He and D'Shay leaned closer.

Humpty whistled. "They got you hard-locked into Canal duty. Hee, hee. Whoa! You hit the jackpot. They got you down for a tunnel sapper."

"A what?"

"Sapper. You crawl on your belly to the raw end of the canal tunnel, drill a hole and poke in explosives. Then you get your ass out before some jerk gets bored and punches the boom-button. Sounds like a rush, don't it."

"Shee-it." D'Shay felt sweat bead on his lip. "Can you make the switch?"

"It'll cost you a thousand."

"A thousand! LaBarre said it'd be seven hundred, max."

Humpty shook his head. "They've got their system locked tighter. And you're a hard case. I gotta skip through a dozen links to beat their trace. This is no routine skim-and-shuffle. Besides, you're black."

"So I've been told. But what's color got to do with price?"

"Some assignment agencies are jumpy about blacks and dusties. They put extra locks on certain jobs. Not my fault, son. I love everybody—long as they pay."

D'Shay knuckled his temples. What if Humpty was a scammer? And if he blew all his cash now there'd be no other chance. But what other options were there? Zip. He took a breath. "Look. I can give you seven hundred now. I can raise the rest by the end of the week. I won't ditch on you."

Humpty scooped a fistful of peanuts from a bowl. "I feel your pain, son." He shrugged. "'Sides, I owe Mr. LaBarre a favor. I'm feeling generous, so the seven hundred now, the rest by Friday."

"Thanks, man."

"None needed. Just remember, I can put you right back to sapper duty—or worse—if you try to skip out on me."

D'Shay nodded. "Yeah, I figured that."

"Okay, so let's see your money."

D'Shay dug a wad of credits from his pocket. The bald man rifled through the bills.

"We're in business. Call me Doc. I think of myself as a data transplant surgeon. One slip, and I lose the patient. But I don't slip."

"Doc it is."

"How long you been a s'teener?"

"Turned seventeen last month."

"Such a tense time for today's youth." He motioned toward the bank of computers. "Okay, let's get to business. Gotta check you out first." He grabbed a laser pen from his desktop. "Time for an iris scan."

D'Shay tried not to blink as the green laser swept his eyes. The computer blipped and spoke in a woman's soft voice. "Confirmation. D'Shay L. Green, age seventeen, three weeks, two days, and six hours."

"Good. Now for some serious data surgery." Doc waggled his fingers and grinned. He spoke to the screen and tapped his vidwand at flashing data levels. After twenty minutes of lightning screen commands, sweat trickled down his cheeks. "Almost there," he said. "Bounced through Paraguay to Uzbekistan. I'm finally in Geneva Headquarters. After I make the final tap, they can trace me in thirty seconds. I'll give you twenty seconds to make a choice before I cut the link. Ready?"

Twenty seconds! Twenty seconds to decide his fate.

Life or death in twenty heartbeats. He wiped his face and nodded. "Okay, I'm ready."

"Showtime!" Doc dove into a blue data layer that displayed a flashing text list.

D'Shay leaned closer and scanned the five choices:

1) Infantry
2) Canal Laborer
3) Sewer works
4) Corridor police
5) SUN colonist/blender

"Tick-tock, the clock is running," said Doc. "Ten, nine, eight—"

"Shit, shit, shit! Okay—the last one! That colonist thing. Just do it!"

Doc hit the com pad. Data swirled and he waved the screen blank. "Excellent choice, m'boy."

"SUN colonist? What the hell's a SUN colonist-slash-blender?"

Doc chewed on a toothpick. "Beats me."

ROOMIES

"There is nowhere you can go and only be with people who are like you. Give it up."

—*Dr. Bernice Johnson Reagon*

On a steamy Friday evening, Jaym and thirty other Corridor s'teeners dragged their duffels off a chartered hydro bus. The bus had taken them deep into the deserted zone of the western Corridor, fenced off from civilians since the Troubles. Now he and the others stood deep within this no-man's land.

Outside the bus they gawked in twilight at the skeletons of high-rises and 'scrapers of the Old Seattle Sector. Even a decade after the Anti-Corp riots the place was still wasted. Beyond the shells of 'scrapers, the twisted column of the Space Needle loomed like a gnarled limb.

"Keep your asses moving!" shouted an Alliance sergeant.

Jaym hefted his duffel and followed other boys darting anxious looks as they filed between rows of unpainted concrete barracks. He stopped at Building A-9 and stepped inside. He glanced at his orders and looked for Bunk 17-B.

There it was, his new home for the next four weeks—a sagging mattress with a rusted iron frame and a battered wall locker. At least he wouldn't have to share it with a day-sleeper.

Anxious-faced s'teeners quietly trickled in to find their places. As Jaym started unpacking his duffle, he noticed an Af-Am in the doorway checking the place out. Jaym fought a jolt of anxiety. *Maybe this Af-Am won't make trouble,* he thought. *Don't make eye contact. Don't be the one to start something.* He tried to act calm as he unfolded socks and underwear. The Af-Am's footsteps approached.

"Nice accommodations," said the black kid. "I'll miss the household rats and perfume of cat piss, but otherwise, not bad." He tossed his duffel on the bunk overhead. "Check out the sheets. Tastefully monogrammed in Magic Marker: 'Property of Global Alliance—N.A.' Nice touch."

Should he say something? But what? And right now his voice would probably be shaky. All he could manage was a half-assed smile and nod as he kept fumbling with socks and underwear. "So, a s'teener of few words." The Af-Am's voice was now flat with a hint of menace. "Okay, bunkmate," sighed the black s'teener. "Let's say we clear the air right now."

Jaym looked up. His voice cracked as he said, "Whaddya mean?"

"You got a problem with skin that's not lily white?"

"Hey, no! It's just that... my hood's had... problems."

"Look. We've both been through some black-white crap," said the Af-Am, "but it'd be best if you and me have a little détente for the next few weeks." He held out a fist. "Name's D'Shay."

"Jaym, Bellvue Sector." They tapped knuckles.

"Bellvue. Sounds like one of those high-end hoods."

"I wish. I'm just a sector rat. No connections, no prospects."

D'Shay nodded. "I feel you. But we're out now. And the Canal didn't get us."

"Where are you assigned?" asked Jaym.

"SUN Colony Service. Africa."

Jaym's hands and insides were no longer shaking. That grip of anxiety had eased. "Huh. Me too. My O.S. designation is 'blender,' whatever that means." He watched D'Shay unpack his duffel. He wasn't like the Af-Am thugs in his sector. D'Shay was about his own size and build. He was lean but muscular, had sharp features, and was lighter-skinned than most Af-Ams he had seen.

D'Shay saw him staring. "Why're you looking at me? You gay?"

Jaym grinned. "No, just curious. Haven't had much contact with Af-Ams."

"I think you're jealous of my perfect skin tone and magnetic good looks. Always makes girls shiver and guys stare in awe."

"I'll do my best to not stare in awe," chuckled Jaym. D'Shay was all right, he thought. Full of himself, but not a cocky bastard looking for trouble. Thank God. D'Shay held out the back of his hand. "Guess you'd call me chocolate-lite. Nice tint, you must admit. Grandma Washington was a hundred percent Af-Am, but Granddad Ramos was Mexican. Don't know about my other grandparents. They died in one of the plagues."

Jaym struggled for something to say. "Been living with your family?"

D'Shay hesitated. "Fostered out a lot. On my own the last few years." He looked away, irritation flickering across his face.

"Your parents dead?"

"Why the third-degree?" D'Shay snapped. "You trying some cross-cultural crap?"

"Hey, no offense, man. Just talking." Damn, thought Jaym. One minute he's grinning and messing around, the next he takes your head off. Is he a schizo?

D'Shay folded rumpled tee shirts and laid them on a locker shelf. "Okay. So how 'bout your family?" His voice was even now. Calmer.

"Only got my Mom."

"How'd she take it? Your assignment and all."

Jaym looked down and fluffed up his flat pillow. "Harder than I expected. I always figured she wanted rid of me. You know, another mouth to feed, and the allotments getting smaller. But she ... she skipped work today and bawled when I left." He still felt a lump in his throat thinking about how she clutched him and sobbed. How he fumbled with words to comfort her. *Maybe it won't be forever*, he had tried. *And, I'll find a way to contact you—to let you know what's going on. You just....* Then he ran out of words and just held her. He hoped she didn't notice his tremble of fear or the welling tears he fought back. "She'll be okay, man. Moms might cry a lot, but they're tough."

The boys were quiet for a moment. Finally D'Shay said, "Hey, do those freckles of yours turn on the ladies?"

Jaym looked at the back of his hands and felt his face flush.

"Lighten up," chuckled D'Shay. "We'll get used to each other." He climbed up to his bunk. "Hee hee. Check out the ceiling roaches. A touch of the old hood. Thoughtful of the Alliance folks."

Heavy bootsteps approached.

Jaym turned to see a gangly Southie staring his way. No, at D'Shay.

The Southie looked toward the other s'teeners and barked, "I need a bunk trade. Ten credits for a swap." Nobody looked up. "Okay, twenty! Twenty, just to sleep near some black fungus."

Jaym's chest tightened.

D'Shay hopped to the floor. He crossed his arms as he spoke low and even. "As I understand the house rules, my tattooed friend—hey, nice swastika—there are no bunk exchanges."

The Southie bared his filed teeth in a menacing grin.

D'Shay waved an arm toward the other s'teeners, all silent. Waiting. "The idea here is for folks to embrace one another's differences. Like the difference between you and me. I'm Af-Am and good looking, while you're a butt-ugly skinhead. But I'm certain that with a little give and take we could—"

36

The Southie dropped his duffel and flashed a serrated shiv. He crouched, waving the knife, edging toward D'Shay.

Jaym slid off his bed, heart drumming. Oh shit. What was he supposed to do? This wasn't his fight. And no way he could tackle a hopped-up Southie with a shiv. But damn, he should do *something*. Maybe move slow and get behind him.

D'Shay glanced at him, shook his head, *no*. Jaym froze. The Southie lunged.

In a blur, D'Shay grabbed the Southie's arm and jacked up his knee. Bones cracked like a snapped broomstick. The knife clattered across the concrete floor. D'Shay shoved the groaning Southie out the door. "Infirmary's to the right." He tossed the duffle outside, then picked up the shiv and slid it under his mattress.

Jaym looked at him wide-eyed.

"Ease up, man. Think I'm gonna stick you?" D'Shay glanced at Jaym. "About the Southie... I can handle myself." He wiped his hands on his jeans. "But I appreciate the offer."

C.A.

Many s'teeners have not had the opportunity to interact with those outside their own districts. In these diversity sessions you will begin to understand and accept cultural differences.

—*Cultural Awareness workshop handout*

Reya assembled for her morning Cultural Awareness session with the other s'teeners in a vast concrete building. S'teeners jostled past, their table assignments in hand, looking for today's C.A. partner. Most looked like plain-vanilla Corridor kids dressed in the Alliance-issued tee shirts and shorts. She saw one other MexiCal girl pass by. They exchanged nods and soft *holas*.

The place was as cozy as a warehouse. It was filled with rows of small, beat-up wooden tables, each with two folding chairs. There were no windows and the cinderblock walls were bare except for the Global Alliance flag up front—a white banner with a circle of seven different colored stars, each representing a region under Alliance control. That same flag had flown over a guard tower at her camp. She hugged herself and looked away. The sight of that flag was a constant reminder that she was trapped, whether it was behind razor wire in the camp, or here in this concrete prison.

Reya hadn't seen a MexiCal flag since she and her family were caught just south of the Corridor. Her mother had brought a hankie-sized flag from home, but a border vigilante tossed it to the ground and heeled it to fragments in the dust.

"All right, people," bellowed the Alliance trainer, a blocky woman about her mom's age. "Let's get moving. Quit milling around and pair up at your assigned table. You should know the drill by now. You've got thirty minutes for each pairing session. Cut any verbal tiptoeing and get to the meat of the assignment. Spill your guts. What you learn from your C.A. partner might help you survive out of country." She glanced at the clock and clapped her hands. "Be sure to fill out the assignment sheet. Okay, let's get to it, people."

These sessions had been numbingly routine for Reya. She had to go through the question-and-answer sheet with Corridor brats who barely made eye contact. It was obvious that no one wanted to spend thirty minutes with a dustie.

She found her table, sat down, and waited. Soon a boy with his assignment sheet paused, then sat across from her. He wasn't bad looking—just pale. He had rusty hair, freckles, and green eyes. Huh. Unlike other Corridor-born, he was actually making eye contact. She noticed his gaze slip to her chest. She crossed her arms. "Tsk, tsk. Eyes up, Corridor Boy."

He glanced to his hands knotted on the desktop.

"Good God, are you blushing?"

He managed a dry cough. "I really wasn't trying to look at—"

"Yes you were. All guys do. But this time I'll give you a pass." She tossed down her assignment sheet. "You know, I'm sick of their mindless Q and A crap. Let's just talk. We'll fill in the blanks with the usual BS."

The boy shrugged. "Fine with me."

"Okay. My name's Reya, and I'm a 'gee."

"Jaym, Bellvue Sector."

"I'm curious, Mr. Jaym. How do you feel about being taken from your cozy hood and your Corridor *chica*?"

Jaym leaned forward, his jaw tight. "Look, I'm not highborn, so I won't miss my hood a bit. I will miss my mom, but no *chica* in my life. No time. I work for our slumlord to pay for tech school and help make rent. Creative work, like painting over graffiti, setting rat traps." He thumbnailed at a heart carved in the tabletop. "How about you. You leave a guy behind?"

"Had to leave my mom and little sister. No guys. Camp life is not conducive to romance. Mostly we work at the camp factory and hustle to make rations." She leaned back, twirling a lock of hair. "I did like one boy who came across the border with us. But last year he got knifed in camp over ration coupons." She snapped her gum and looked away. *Don't cry now*, she thought. *Not in front of this Corridor boy.*

They sat quietly. She picked at a raw hangnail.

He finally asked, "What about your mom and sister? Will they get out?"

Reya squeezed her eyes shut. "Leeta might when she's a s'teener—if she survives camp. Seven more years. Mom said she's gonna stay alive to protect Leeta. But then..." She wiped an escaped tear. "Shit. I only wish I could return for Leeta's *quinceañera*."

"Her what?"

"Her *quinceañera*! Do you gringos know nothings?" she said in a just-across-the-border accent.

Jaym made a half smile.

"It's the big turning-fifteen celebration for MexiCal girls. Their initiation to womanhood."

"Did you have a... Keensierra?"

"Not like the one I had dreamed for. My *quinceañera* passed in the mountains, trekking north. That night, after the men and boys bedded down, my aunt and cousins gave me ribbons, a pair of earrings. Leeta gave me her lucky agate from the old farm."

"Hey," Jaym said softly, "Only five minutes left. We better do something for the assignment."

Reya wiped an eye and looked at her sheet. "Yeah, okay I'm gonna be a blender—seems we all are. I'm assigned to Mizambu on the southeast African coast. Great beaches in Mizambu, they say. I'll be a med-tech dosing out gene therapy in highland villages."

Jaym's eyes widened. "A med-tech? Really?"

"Oh, I forgot. We 'gees are uneducated lowlifes, right?"

"No, no. I mean I've only seen the camp. Heard talk." He knuckled his chin.

She sniffed. "So what's your service?" she asked.

"I'll be doing hydro in Africa. Thought I'd get short-term service, five to eight years max." He crossed his arms and looked away. "But I guess being a blender is a life sentence."

"My God, boy. It's a fresh start! You get out of this rat hole of a Corridor, and I'm out of 'gee camp—without Canal duty! How lucky is that?" She looked past Jaym, her eyes bright. "I can't wait. No fences, no walls. Bet Mizambu even has monkeys and butterflies. Can you imagine? Real butterflies."

"Yeah, but do you wanna live out your life in some African village? They'll take our help, but we'll always be outsiders."

She shook her head slowly. "You don't have a clue why we're going over there, do you? You've got no idea what blenders really do."

"It's no big mystery. We're gonna use our training to try to salvage a piece of Africa. You'll use your med-tech skills, and I'll work hydro."

Reya held up a hand and leaned closer. "You really think that's it? The only thing blenders do?"

Jaym shrugged. "Is there some shit work they haven't told us about? Please don't tell me they're digging a canal over there too."

She shook her head and spoke softly. "Here's a hint, Jaymo: '*Blending* Program.' Think hard now."

Jaym frowned. "Okay, we're blending with the population so we can—." His eyes widened.

"Bingo," said Reya. "SUN has paired each of us with our African soul mate. An arranged DNA wedding. But with a little luck, you'll get a babe, and I'll get a stud...so to speak."

"So, why haven't the manuals said anything about this?"

She shrugged. "Probably so some of us don't freak out, like you're doing right now, and try to go AWOL."

"But why should Africans let us ... 'blend' with them? And what's the point? Since it's a life assignment, I figured I'd pair up with one of our own kind—another blender."

"What's the point? Haven't you heard of the Eleven-Effect?"

"No."

"It's in chapter 14 of the *Blender's Handbook*."

"That was just historical stuff. Wars, plagues, coups, and climate change."

"That 'historical stuff' is going to shape the rest of your life. Remember the solar flare of '58?"

"Sure. But it was the middle of the night here. I was only six or seven, but I remember. I thought they were giant ghosts dancing in the sky. Scared the crap out of me."

"NorthAm lucked out, but Africa took the brunt of the flare. It not only fried people outright, but African survivors had every cell in their body zapped by nasty particles. No obvious internal damage for most survivors, but the long-term effects are caused by breaks in their Chromosome-11. You've had biology, right?"

"Sure."

"Well, the Eleven-Effect is recessive, so it would cause no harm on its own. But when two Elevens cross—any flare-exposed African male and female—the fetus gets scrambled and you're guaranteed a miscarriage. Africans are gonna die out unless they mix with outsiders not exposed to the flare. That's us. Africans need our healthy Elevens."

"Why not use gene therapy? Or ship over donor sperms and eggs?"

She shook her head. "Did you study about the Troubles in school?"

"Yes. Food riots, religious nuts blowing up research labs and burning universities."

"Yeah, the crazies went underground after the Global Alliance forces got nasty with them. Rumor is that rebels are still making bombs and assassinating scientists and profs. So it's gonna take decades to get gene technology back. But Africa can't wait. In a couple of decades women will be past childbearing age and, poof, Africans will die out."

Jaym rubbed his forehead, thinking. *Damn, I'm gonna have to live in a hut and eat stir-fried beetles. No choice of who I get paired up with. Be surrounded by an African family that speaks Swahili or something.*

"Feeling sorry for yourself?" asked Reya. "Well, you poor, poor baby." She snapped her fingers. "Lemme see your blender match."

"Whaddya mean?"

"On your holo-card."

He unclipped the plastic card from his shirt and handed it over.

Reya tapped the card to life. She tilted it, scanning through the rainbow of data layers. "You've never checked out Level-16? The stuff past your vitals and schooling?"

"Not much point. Everything past Level-9 is a tangle of Alliance rules and regulations."

"Try to be less clueless. If you showed a little curiosity you'd see a preview of your blending match. Always dig deeper, Jaymo, or you're gonna have a dull future." She tapped the edge of the card several times with her fingernail. "Here we go. Your African *chica* is 'L. Zingali.' Says she's one-point-five meters tall. Short, but her height-weight ratio is good. Her DNA alert only shows the Eleven-Effect. Huh. Under 'education' it notes she's had 'extended schooling.'" Reya handed back the holo-card. "She sounds like a catch."

Jaym stared at the card, numb. This piece of plastic had the rest of his life mapped out—and the life of some African girl. God, how could he ever—

Reya slapped her hand on the table. "Snap out of it!"

Jaym jerked up in his chair.

Reya's mouth was tight, her eyes flashed. "The dice have come up good for you and you can't even see that! It's freedom. You got a great pick and we're gonna get outta this Corridor cage. So spit it out. What's your real problem?"

"It's just that—I grew up here. It's all I know. I could take getting shipped to Africa for a few years, if I knew

I was coming back...but to be a lifer with a village girl who'll probably hate my guts..."

Reya stood, slammed the chair against the table, and stormed away.

"Hey, wait. I'm..."

NOVO ESPERO

As a Blender, you will be transported to your overseas destination on a safe, clean, efficient vessel. The Global Alliance has contracted with GlobeTran, Ltd. for your transportation. Enjoy your voyage and exciting new assignment.

—*Blender Handbook, p. 13*

D'Shay and Jaym wedged through the crowd of dockside s'teeners toward the shade of their towering transport ship. Jaym noticed that everyone had been issued the same new outfits: khaki tee shirts and shorts, thick-soled sandals, and formless brimmed hats of canvas that could be folded and stuffed in one of the flapped pockets of shorts or crammed in a backpack. The hats were no fashion statement, but kept the sun off your face and neck, and the grommeted holes allowed for some air circulation. And thank God for the light-adjusting sunglasses.

D'Shay dropped his pack and flapped air under his tee shirt.

"You think this is hot?" said Jaym. "Wait till we get to Africa."

"Come off it, Jaymo. There's gonna be tropical breezes, fresh air, and maybe even real rain." D'Shay scanned the rusted bow of their transport, trying to decipher the original name painted over in gray. Pale red letters bled through in places. He pieced together, *Vlostok II*. Probably a Russian transport retrofitted from the petro era. Stenciled just above the painted-out name, *Novo Espero* glowed neon blue. He elbowed Jaym. "My WorldSpeak sucks. What's the name mean?"

"Something like, 'New Spirit,' maybe 'New Dawn.'"

D'Shay chuckled. "*Rust Bucket* must not have been in the WorldSpeak dictionary." He pointed to metal patches riveted near the water line. "Check it out. She took a hit or two in the wars. Tough old gal."

"How come they don't use cargo planes to get us over there?" asked Jaym.

"They only use cargo planes for military transport. A ship is safer. Didn't you hear about that AirTrain last month?"

Jaym shook his head.

"Word is, an RPG barbecued eight hundred British troops before they got off the runway. Any freak with a shoulder-launched missile can take down a cargo plane."

Jaym frowned and recalled the MexiCal girl telling about renegades and terrorists still on the loose. A harsh, but good-looking girl. What was her name? Reesa? No, Reya. Wonder if he'd see her on board. She sure had been pissed during their C.A. encounter.

He wandered to the dock's edge. The dark water lapped

slowly against the pilings. A few dead fish rocked back and forth in the shallow waves. The water was swirled with oil slicks that shown like greasy rainbows. The stench of rotted fish and oil nearly made him gag.

A loudspeaker crackled. "Attention colonists. Prepare to board. Sector hoods and refugees will be mixed aboard ship. There will be *no* exchange of assignments. Your ship, the crew, and guards are provided by GlobeTran, Limited.

The speaker voice continued. "Once you are onboard, the GlobeTran captain of the *Novo Espero* and his guards have full authority from Global Alliance to administer military justice on the high seas."

"Guess we play nice or walk the plank," said D'Shay.

The loudspeaker barked again. "Listen up. When your number is called, step to the boarding ramp."

"Charlie-94 and Alpha-105." S'teeners began to shuffle forward.

D'Shay was one of the first to be called. "See you aboard, Jaymo." He elbowed past sweaty arms and jogged up the ramp. At the hatchway a pock-faced G-T guard glanced at his ID tag, checked his clipboard, and muttered, "Down the first stairwell. Deck-3, Bay-19. Move out."

D'Shay's assigned bunk already had been claimed. As he looked around he realized no one seemed to pay attention to bunk assignments, and apparently the guards didn't care. So friends stayed with friends, and people tended to cluster with members of their own hoods.

Jaym and D'Shay found each other and scouted out three empty bunks in the niche of a bulkhead toward the stern. "Not bad," said D'Shay, tossing his pack on the unoccupied third bunk.

Jaym nodded. "A little cramped, but out of the traffic of the mob. A private suite for our voyage."

———

When the *Novo Espero* pulled away from the dock, Jaym, D'Shay, and the other blenders were allowed topside to watch the hazed buildings of the Corridor fade into the distance. The ship glided across the blue-gray of the Pacific, gently lifting and falling with the swells. "Whoa," said Jaym. "I feel kind of…weird. Sort of dizzy."

"Called seasickness," chuckled D'Shay. "Gotta get your sea legs. Just don't think about it. It's mental, Jaymo."

"Right," said Jaym. "See you…below." He rubber-legged his way to the stairwell.

———

The third day out, all passengers were confined below as the *Novo Espero* was slammed by ten-meter waves from a typhoon blasting from the southwest. Jaym clutched his bunk, fighting the waves of nausea. D'Shay, however, lay in his bunk, numb with boredom as he again paged through the crumbled graphic novel he found wedged behind his mattress. The text was Russian, the story bloody and tragic, but the girls were hot with their torn blouses and crotch-high skirts. At least it helped pass the endless hours in the dim lighting of Deck-3. After his fourth or fifth read, he tossed the graphic aside and hopped to the floor. "Hey, Jaymster," he said, gripping a girder as the ship rocked. "I'm going for a stroll around the neighborhood. Want me to grab you a new barf bag?"

Jaym moaned. "No thanks. Actually, I haven't hurled for an hour."

"Great. Bet you're ready for some cruise-liner cuisine. How about I bring you a plate of powdered eggs, scrambled nice and runny."

Jaym put his face in his pillow.

"Or maybe a glop of greasy gravy poured tastefully over a stale biscuit? Ummm. Or perhaps—"

"Just go 'way."

D'Shay chuckled and headed for the central bays. He was getting good at balancing and anticipating the pitching and rolling of the ship, only occasionally needing to grab a bunk post for support—usually when the vessel unexpectedly yawed to one side. He noticed that even the crew grabbed for something when the deck tilted too far for comfort.

He wove his way between bay aisles. Too bad, he thought, that blenders had taken bunks with s'teeners from their own hoods. Af-Am guys bunked in one section; the girls in another near them. Same with the whites. Here we were, all heading off to be blenders, but can't even do a little blending on shipboard.

One common bond all were forced to share was the aroma of Deck-3. Barf, sweat, and the rank smell wafting from the clogged-up latrines. One would think the Globe-Tran folks would take a little more pride in their service. At least loan us a plunger.

D'Shay paused by a group of Af-Am guys tossing dice against a bulkhead. One looked up. "Want in, brother?"

"Nah. Never had any luck with the cubes."

"Come on, my man. Can't be any worse than me." The bare-chested boy said, "I've lost my shirt in this game!" D'Shay noticed one of them elbow another.

D'Shay sighed. "Okay, okay. Guess I got nothing better to do. How much to get in the game?" Thirty minutes later D'Shay smiled as he walked away with winnings bulging his pocket.

Heading to the latrine he watched a group of white girls working on each other's hair like monkeys picking nits. They were trying to twine their locks into cornrows, but they just made crooked rows of stubble. They must be trying to achieve an African look, he thought. As if a white girl with cornrows could better fit into an African crowd.

The girls stopped when they saw him watching.

"What!" snapped one of them, a blonde with black roots showing through.

"Your effort is all well and good," said D'Shay, "but you might consult with an expert, like one of those ladies." He pointed to Af-Am girls laughing at something in the next bay.

Blondie narrowed her eyes. "Bite me," she hissed.

"Tsk, tsk. You might want to work on your interpersonal skills before you get to your assignment."

"You want your ass kicked back to your black bay? We know guys in the next section who would be happy to escort you." The other girls laughed.

D'Shay just grinned, shook his head, then walked to the latrine.

A girl rushing from the woman's side almost collided with D'Shay. "Watch where you're going!" she snapped, shouldering past.

D'Shay watched her disappear into the bays. *A dustie?* he thought. *Huh!* He'd heard most were shipped straight from their 'gee camps to the Canal. Good-looking girl. Straight black hair, a hint of Mayan or Aztec in those strong facial bones. Weird, she was the only dustie he'd seen aboard.

When he returned to their ductwork suite, Jaym was sitting on his bunk, face still pale, but he managed a weak grin. "I think the ocean has settled down—thank God." He stood, holding his bunk post. "I gotta make it to the latrine."

D'Shay grabbed an overhead pipe and began a set of chin-ups. "Funny thing—I ran into a dustie girl coming out of the latrine. Still can't believe she's a blender."

"Oh, yeah? I think I know who she is," said Jaym. "Yes, she's a genuine blender. We had a C.A. session together in training. Just don't ever call her a 'dustie' or she'll take your head off."

"Fine looking lady," said D'Shay, dropping back to the floor.

"Her name's Reya. But I'm on her shit list after our C.A. session. Thinks I'm a racist."

"Maybe you just need a tutorial on dealing with the ladies, Jaymster."

"I'll keep that in mind." He let go of the post and wobbled toward the latrine.

But halfway there he froze at the sound of a muffled scream in the shadow of a stairwell. Two white boys had a girl pushed against a steel grate. The one behind her had her arms pinned. The boy with a buzz cut had his hand clapped over her mouth and was groping under her tee shirt. She kicked and bucked, but the boys had her locked down.

It was her, Reya. He hesitated a moment. Crap! Those guys will wipe the deck with me, he thought. Oh, hell. Jaym yelled and charged. He jumped the groper from behind. His arm wrapped around the boy's throat and yanked him to the floor. They rolled, kicking and hitting.

Jaym gasped at the red flash and stunning pain. *The other guy.* Jaym saw the blur of the boot again but rolled, still locked with Buzz-Cut. The full blow caught Buzz-Cut in the face. The boy screamed and swore, crawling from Jaym's grip.

Suddenly the other kid fell hard to the deck, moaning and clutching his groin. Reya then stomped him on the side of his head.

Jaym got to his knees. She helped him stand.

"You ... okay?" Jaym asked.

She nodded, straightening her tee shirt. "Thanks, I ... Hey, I know you. We were in C.A. together and you were—"

"The class asshole," finished Jaym.

She half grinned. "Close enough."

D'Shay jogged toward them. "What the hell... Your nose looks like a mashed tomato, Jaymster."

"Jaymster?" asked Reya.

"Just Jaym, please."

"Oh, yeah. I'm Reya, if you've forgotten."

Jaym nodded. "I remember."

"Okay, what went down here?" asked D'Shay.

"As one of the few 'gees on board," said Reya, "I guess these two slimes thought I was fair game to be their plaything." She turned to the dozens of s'teeners watching. "Hey, assholes!" she shouted. "Thanks for all the help!"

Most turned away and headed back to their bays.

"Where's your bunk?" asked D'Shay.

"I was in Bay-6 down at the end. But I got exiled to a corner by some Anglo girls."

"We've got an extra bunk in our bay. I think you should stick with us."

Jaym nodded. "We're harmless."

"Here," said Reya, handing Jaym a wad of toilet paper. "Your nose is still bleeding."

When they reached their bunks D'Shay said, "Your accommodations, ma'am."

Reya tossed her pack on the spare bunk. "You guys better be as harmless as you say. I know some unpleasant tricks in case one of you tries something."

"Don't worry about me, baby," said D'Shay. "It's Jaymo there you should watch."

Her dark eyes narrowed. "Don't call me baby," she said. "Ever!"

"Hey, just trying to be pleasant. No disrespect, okay? I come in peace." He held out a fist.

She glared, but finally tapped his knuckles. "Yeah, okay. Peace."

"So, you're a 'gee."

She straightened her back, fists on hips. "Got a problem with that?"

"Hey, no. My hood's crappy, but you 'gees … Glad you got out, girl."

She looked at Jaym, sitting on his bunk still trying to staunch his bleeding nose. "Lemme see the nose." He pulled away the wad of bloody tissue and she fingered the bridge of his nose. "It's broken. I'm going to reset it, so hold on to the bunk pole. This will be fast."

"But—"

Snap.

"Oh God that hurt!"

"Lie flat for a while. You'll live."

"Damn. How'd you learn to do that?" asked D'Shay.

"I had some med-tech training before we came north. Probably why I made the Blender list."

"Thanks be that we have a doctor in our presence," said D'Shay with a grin. "We'd better make an offering to the sea god—old What's-His-Name."

Reya smiled. "His name's Neptune. The old guy with a seaweed beard and a trident."

"A *try dent?*"

"Trident, one word. It's like a pitchfork."

"Where'd you learn all this stuff, Dr. Reya?"

She twisted a lock of hair. "You gotta promise not to laugh, okay?"

"Promise," said D'Shay.

"Jaym?"

He nodded and mumbled through his tissue wad. "I promise."

Reya sat on her bunk and took a breath. "I learned a lot from my *abuela*—my grandma. She had a roomful of books, some English, some Spanish. She taught school before the dunes came. When I was little, the night winds howled like ghosts and grit tapped at my window like fingernails. When I'd cry, Grandma would come in and hold me, tell me stories. She liked stories with gods and fairies. Aztec, Greek, Roman—didn't matter to her. Anyway, Neptune and his singing mermaids were one of her stories."

"Your grandma still in 'gee camp?" asked D'Shay.

Reya shook her head. "She disappeared one night in the Sierras. Too rocky to track her. She knew there wasn't enough food for us all."

The three lay quiet in the dim glow of flickering deck lights.

———

By Day Four the storm eased up and s'teeners were allowed topside for two hours a day. None of the other blenders bothered them again. In fact, some nodded respectfully to

Reya or one of the boys. When on deck, some blenders took shelter from the wind behind huge ventilation stacks. Others stood at the rail, squinting into the wind and salt spray from white caps.

Today Jaym, Reya, and D'Shay leaned on the rail and looked at the expanse of ocean fading into a far mist.

"I love this," said Reya, sweeping her arm toward the horizon. "Must be a billion cubic kilometers of water out here."

"Yeah," said Jaym. "You'd think the brains in the Global Alliance could figure out how to desalinate some for Mexi-Cal."

"I think the Alliance can barely hold itself together, let alone do something that useful," said Reya. She pointed toward the bow. "Hey, guys, look—an albatross!"

D'Shay shook his head. "That's just a big seagull."

"A seagull with a four-meter wingspan?" She watched the bird effortlessly glide just above the waves. "It has absolute freedom. It can skim the oceans its entire life." She whispered, "No fences, no walls."

Jaym gripped the rail as the ship rose slowly then slid over a swell. "The ocean is pretty awesome, but so much water gives me the creeps. There's nothing to orient you out here—no street grids; no buildings."

D'Shay nodded. "I feel you, man. I'll be glad to set my feet on asphalt again."

Reya shook her head. "Not sure if Africa has asphalt."

"Asphalt, gravel—all better than being out here," said D'Shay. "Bet we're over kilometers of cold water."

"More like ten or twenty," said Jaym.

"That's it. I'm going below," said D'Shay. "You're freaking me out."

———

During the following days Reya taught them a MexiCal card game called *Conquian*. Jaym didn't know any games, but picked up D'Shay's variation on seven-card stud and cleaned him out of toothpicks. They talked about their assignments, practiced a little WorldSpeak, and pored over a tattered map of East Africa that Reya copped from a ship's bulletin board.

Then one afternoon after lunch, Reya signaled D'Shay and Jaym to go topside with her.

"What's up?" asked Jaym, clambering up the stairwell after her.

"Not yet. We can't be overheard."

It was a cloudy day and the rolling swells were an iron gray. Thunderclouds had piled on the horizon, but the ship was heading southeast, toward sunlit ocean. Reya took the boys to the ship's stern. It was chilly with a steady breeze. Most blenders were below. The three had the stern to themselves.

"Guys, I overheard a couple of crew laughing about how we blenders are going to run into some surprises not mentioned in the *Blender's Handbook*."

"Surprises?" asked D'Shay. "Like what?"

"No hints," said Reya. "Look, I think we'll be fine, but if something goes wrong for any one of us..."

"Like if the Blending program is a scam?" asked Jaym. "Like maybe the Corridor has arranged to dump us in Africa just to get rid of us?"

"No way," said D'Shay. "Be easier just to send us to the Canal."

"Look," said Reya. "I'm just saying, if things go bad for any reason, we should have a way to contact each other if we run into trouble. We could warn or help each other—if we can."

"Fine, but how?" said D'Shay.

"We should have a rendezvous point, a place to find each other, just in case."

"Okay," said Jaym, "but where and how?"

Reya unfolded her small Blender map of East Africa.

"We're landing here," she said, tapping a bay.

"Bonique City in Mizambu," said Jaym. "You're assigned near there, right?"

She nodded. "Somewhere north in the highlands, about here. And you guys are going west to Chewena." Her finger traced a twisting crosshatched line. "You'll probably take this rail line to the capital, Wananelu. Looks like about 150 klicks from Bonique City."

"Okay," said D'Shay. "You're there, we're here. Then what?"

"D'Shay," she said, "you're our best bet as a contact. You're assigned to Wananelu, about 100,000 people. Jaym and I are gonna be in villages, probably with no com links.

You'll have a real address, maybe even an in-house com line. You'll be our main contact."

"Fine by me," said D'Shay.

"And Jaym, from what we can tell from your assignment data, you're gonna be maybe twenty klicks from D'Shay. So, D'Shay, when you get a chance, make it out to Jaym's village. It'll be easier for you to find Jaym than for him to try to track you down in the big city. What's the name of your village?"

Jaym glanced at his assignment card. "Nis—Nswibe. About twenty klicks north-northwest of Wananelu."

"So, D'Shay, when you get a break, find Jaym and give him your address and a com number, if your place has one."

"What about you?" D'Shay asked her. "How do we reach you?"

"I'll contact one of you guys somehow; probably you, Jaym, assuming I can get a letter to your village. When the three of us get each other's locations, we'll decide on our Plan-B meet-up site. Let's just hope we don't need to use it."

Jaym and D'Shay nodded.

"Good," said Reya. "Okay. We'll exchange assignment data and tuck it away. Agreed?"

They rapped knuckles. "All for one, and one for all," said D'Shay.

AFRICA

Since the chaos of the Pan-Af Wars, and the
following plague years of the early 2050s, much
order has been restored in East Africa. However,
rebels continue to disrupt the goals of the Global
Alliance. Our African-based contractor, GlobeTran,
Ltd., assures us that they are launching an all-out
effort to stamp out rebel strongholds.

—*Global Alliance internal memo*

On Day Ten at sea, a boy clambered down the stairs
and shouted, "There's seagulls on the rail!"

"Land ahoy!" hollered D'Shay. "Hallelujah!"

The intercom boomed: *"Attention colonists. Return to
your berths. Stow your belongings for disembarkation at 1400
hours."*

Jaym sat quietly on the edge of his bunk, a wadded
tee shirt clutched in his fist. In just minutes he'd step on
African soil and he knew he'd never leave again. He'd never
see Mom and might never know what happened to her.
And what about the talk that Reya overheard? Maybe there
really wasn't a SUN Program. What if the Global Alliance

had something sinister up its sleeve for blenders? But what could that be?

"Hey, Jaymo," said Reya. "You okay?"

"Uh, yeah … I'm good." He finished cramming his duffle. "Just … you know—a little nervous I guess."

"Get *excited!* Our new start!"

They finished packing and tossing sheets and pillowcases into the hampers the crew had rolled out. Jaym noticed most passengers sat on their bare bunks in silence, each in their own thoughts.

Twenty minutes later the intercom barked, *"Begin disembarkation. Decks One and Two, file out in bay order."*

Reya grinned. "Never forget, we're gonna get in touch."

Jaym nodded. "Right, Plan-B."

"Come on, Jaymster," said D'Shay. "This is gonna be good. Do I have to kick your butt to make you see that?"

"Sorry, guys. I know it'll be better once we start moving and we actually see Africa. Maybe I just need to get off this hulk and get grounded."

Thirty minutes later the intercom announced, *"Decks Three through Five, disembark now!"*

———

Jaym clattered up corroded stairs with the flow of blenders. Each deck reeked of barf, B.O., and disinfectant. He climbed fast, trying to stay with Reya, who took the stairs two at a time.

Yes, he thought. It will be good, at least better. Has

to be. And in just seconds he'd gulp fresh air—air sweet with tropical flowers. The sea breeze would cool his face. There! Just ahead. Blinding sunlight through the hatch. He jogged the last few steps to the deck.

The heat slammed him; sucked the air from his lungs. Like being smothered by a steaming blanket. "Jesus," he muttered.

Reya squinted. "Whoa! Like a MexiCal summer, with a sauna bonus."

Crewmembers herded them single file down the bouncing gangway. On the dock, Jaym gasped at the harbor stench of bilge oil and rot.

"I ... thought there'd be blue water," whispered Reya. "Kids swimming."

Jaym squinted across the harbor where the hulks of half-sunk ships jutted like jagged rocks. Beyond those loomed the haze of a seaport—a gray-brown sprawl of stained concrete buildings, rusting cranes, squatty warehouses. Some buildings had been reduced to piles of rubble, while others stood severed, or leaned with gaping wounds. Had to be from the Pan-Af Wars.

At the harbor's edge a hill of garbage rose seven or eight stories high. Trash miners, like a swarm of ants, picked their ways across the mound.

More s'teeners crowded onto the dock, pressing Jaym and the others forward. Near the crowd of blenders a flag hung limp, its red, green, and yellow bands faded by the African sun.

Jaym dropped his pack and mopped his face. He glanced

up at a watchtower where a guard took a lazy drag on his cigarette and scanned the gathered colonists. The man's shade was a frayed TUBORG BEER beach umbrella. He stubbed out his cigarette, picked up a clipboard and hoisted a megaphone.

"Listen up colony peoples. I read assignment numbers once only. Okay, Assignments 1 through 464 assemble to platform A."

Reya's eyes widened. "That's me! I'm 134." She looked around. "Hey, Jaym. Where's D'Shay?"

He craned his neck to scan the herd of jostling s'teeners. "He can't be far."

"Well, damn. I'd hoped we three could say goodbye together. Tell D'Shay goodbye for me." She gave him a quick hug and shouldered her pack.

Jaym made a crooked smile.

"Chin up, Jaymo." Suddenly she was swallowed into the mass of shuffling passengers.

Jaym stood amid the swarm of blenders, but was surprised at the emptiness he felt with Reya gone. Soon D'Shay would leave and Jaym would have no one. Funny, he thought, in the few days they had spent together he grew so close to them—maybe what brothers and sisters felt.

"Hey, Jaymster," shouted D'Shay, wedging through the crowd. "Figured you fell off the dock." D'Shay glanced around. "Where's our spicy *chicana?*"

"Just left."

"Damn. Gonna miss that girl."

"Numbers 465 through 600 report to platform G."

D'Shay checked his assignment card. "Whoa—that's me. SUN requires my services. Well, Sir Jaymster, it's—"

"Not so fast," said Jaym. He double-checked his number. "We're gonna be together a while longer."

They worked their way through crowds of s'teeners to platform G. From there a cordon of guards funneled them to a train siding. Guards checked their ID cards and pointed to a peeling, green passenger car. Inside the baking-hot car they claimed a wooden bench and tossed their packs in the overhead.

"Maybe I should tell the conductor they forgot to turn on the AC," said D'Shay.

"Yeah. And when you do, ask for two big glasses of SpringPür, extra ice." He plopped on the bench and scanned the windows, the graffitied walls. Had to be a pre-war metro coach. From the smell of exhaust drifting in open windows, the engine had to run on some kind of petrochem. The el-mags probably froze up years ago. The fumes were choking, but the sun beat too hot to close the windows. No chance anyway. Half were just empty frames. The few remaining panes were cracked or pocked with bullet holes.

Within twenty minutes the car was half filled with s'teeners. After another thirty sweltering minutes, the train jerked forward. They moved past the trash mountain, the rubble of buildings, shantytown shacks, and then headed into rolling countryside.

D'Shay stretched out on an empty bench and yawned. He tucked his tee shirt under his head and closed his eyes. "Nap time, Jaymo."

Jaym glanced at the others in the car—about two dozen in all, plus the single guard wearing a GlobeTran uniform. The man stood with one foot braced on a bench as he scanned the countryside. A stubby automatic hung at his side. He only moved to shoo a fly or to drag on his cigarette.

D'Shay snored softly as the train chuffed across scrubby savanna and past scattered settlements. Most villages in this area looked like they'd been torched. Jaym's *Orientation Handbook* included a brief paragraph on the Pan-Af Wars, but only mentioned that soldiers and mercenaries had looted and burned across much of southeastern Africa. It also said vast regions of the continent were hit by disease and were still depopulated. With so many unburied bodies, diseases erupted and mutated. Where infections had hit hard, med-teams were forced to incinerate homes and entire villages. Hundreds of med-tech workers died before new antivirals could be developed.

The train stopped at the few inhabited villages along the way to unload sacks of grain. At some stops one or two colonists got off, ID tags out, their faces tense. Jaym's gut tightened as he watched them standing on the platform like abandoned kids. And he'd be one of them soon.

The railroad grade rose gradually into low hill country, now high enough for him to catch glimpses of peaks, blue in the distance. Real mountains! And the sky—an impossibly deep blue, almost purple. Another miracle was the air. Between wafts of engine exhaust, he tasted sweet air that didn't sting eyes, didn't burn lungs.

Further on, the train clacked over a bridge spanning a

knife-edge canyon. At the bottom rushed tumbling white water—nothing like the sluggish, algae-clogged rivulets of the Corridor.

He shook D'Shay awake.

"Hey—what's happenin'?" He squinted at Jaym. "We there already?"

Jaym waved toward the windows. "You're missing it! My God, look out there. The rivers are full and fast, and the sky—it's like it's painted. Those trees are thick with leaves. And over there. Flowers."

D'Shay shook his head. "Gotta be litter."

"No, man. And check out the birds. Look, there's a whole flock across the field. Yellow birds—and there, those big white birds with legs like stilts! There must be—"

"Okay, okay. I'm impressed. Looks like Africa's supposed to look." He leaned back and closed his eyes.

SCREEEEEEE!

The train lurched. D'Shay banged to the floor; Jaym was thrown to his hands and knees.

S'teeners screamed.

Locked wheels shrieked on the rails. Guards shouted and leaped from the train.

Gunfire chattered. Shouts.

Windows popped and shattered. Bullets whizzed like bees. Jaym sprawled flat on the floor. D'Shay and others crawled under benches. Diamonds of glass showered benches and the backs of cowering s'teeners.

Then, silence. Only the cries of startled birds and shouts of guards.

Jaym crawled through broken glass to an open window. He eased high enough to see guards yelling, pointing toward a deep grove of trees. More gunfire chattered as they raked the stand of woods. The guards stopped and listened. The brassy litter of shell casings glinted in the harsh sunlight. The sulfur stink of gunpowder drifted through shattered windows.

A girl stuttered, "Are w-we gonna die?"

"What the hell's going on?" asked D'Shay, hunkered low.

"Can't tell," said Jaym. "Shooters in a grove of trees, but I can't see anybody."

With guns pointed at the grove, the guards backed up to the train. One shouted at s'teeners peering from the broken windows. *"Korecte. Es okay, Korecte."* Guards rolled away logs blocking the track.

In minutes the train jerked and started moving. The guards jumped aboard and positioned themselves beside windows, rifles poised. The train picked up speed and pulled away. Jaym waited, but no more shots. Soon they were snaking up the grade of a narrow canyon, a swift river tumbling far below. One by one the passengers got up and wiped glass from the benches.

"Damn," muttered D'Shay. "So 'gades aren't just a fairy tale. There's more than birds and flowers to watch for."

"You suppose Reya's gonna be okay?" asked Jaym.

"If anybody's gonna be okay, it's Lady Reya."

Jaym nodded as he fingered a splintered bullet hole in his bench.

WANANELU

Wananelu (Wun-AHN-uh-loo), capital of
Chewena, South East Africa. A series of Life-
Presidents ran the country until the 2056 Civil
War, when it fell into chaos for a decade. Global
Alliance troops established a governing council in
2064. Estimated population in 2065 was 120,000,
down from its high of 780,000.

—*Global Alliance Gazetteer, p. 864*

D'Shay leaned out the window as the train skirted a
vast turquoise lake speckled with whitecaps. The
wind off the lake felt so good in this heat, but the train
clacked west, passing through low hills dotted with more
and more villages. Many had been burned, but in one village a dozen children ran out to wave at the train. D'Shay
grinned and waved back. As they passed a green adobe
tavern, the men out front hurled beer bottles toward the
train. A couple of men held out fists and shouted.

Jaym hung out the window next to D'Shay. "Suppose
those are welcome-to-Chewena shouts?"

"Wouldn't count on it."

They passed larger villages. Soon a road paralleled the tracks, but only a few bicycles and pedestrians traveled the rough asphalt. A burnt-out personnel carrier lay vine-covered in a ditch.

S'teeners leaned out to crane ahead as they approached the city.

"Check out the stadium," said D'Shay. Artillery shells had pocked the concrete amphitheater, yet a few tattered banners still rimmed the top deck. Now came clusters of rail-side shacks, and within minutes they were passing a shamble of apartment buildings and high-rise offices. Except for a few obvious artillery holes in their sides, most still stood.

"Not as bad as Bonique City, Jaymster. I think we can handle this."

Jaym was quiet, looking at the buildings and staring at locals.

They braced as the train squealed and pulled into the depot. A peeling plywood sign announced:

WANANELU STACIO
WANANELU STATION

D'Shay grabbed his pack. "Our stop. Come on, Jaymo."

They and six other s'teeners stepped out to the depot platform. All had donned their Alliance-issued hats and sunglasses against the searing African sun. Jaym looked at the other blenders in their khaki tee shirts and shorts, all being stared at by passing Africans. He wondered why the

Alliance couldn't be a little more creative in giving them clothing that didn't scream, *here stands a group of clueless clones from another planet.*

Between the blenders and the whitewashed depot ran a cobbled street busy with Africans on foot. There were shoeless old men in frayed clothing, one pushing a broom in the gutter. A heavyset businessman passed in a sweat-stained shirt and striped tie. Within a minute a group of ribby boys pressed the s'teeners with pleading eyes and outstretched hands. "Sorry kids," said D'Shay. "No handouts from us. We don't have anything to give. *Comprende?* Instead of backing off, the kids' hands were all over D'Shay's clothing, trying to snap open pockets and unbuckle his pack. "Back off!" shouted D'Shay, pushing away the taller kids.

While D'Shay was being swarmed, Jaym noticed a group of chattering young mothers toting babies wrapped in colorful backcloths.

"Hey," he said. "Check it out. Those women have babies!"

D'Shay broke free of the kids and gawked. "But they can't. The Eleven-Effect." He trotted toward the women. They began to run. "'Scuse me ladies, wait. I just want to ask—"

One of the babies bounced free of a backcloth.

"No!" shouted D'Shay.

The baby somersaulted in the air, then fell toward the pavement. D'Shay made a diving catch.

The women kept running, not even looking back. With

elbows and knees skinned, D'Shay lay on his back and stared at the button eyes, hair of yarn, sewn canvas skin.

———

With no one on the platform to greet them, the s'teeners decided to try the depot. Inside a neon "Drink AfriCola" sign sputtered above the snack bar where the cook scraped his grill. The smell of fried meat mixed with the stink of urine from the open restroom. Fat flies bumbled at the single window in the "dining" area, which consisted of two plywood tables with shaky-looking rattan chairs. D'Shay spotted a GlobeTran soldier sitting at a corner table. She wore khakis and a blue beret—a good-looking African woman in her thirties with strong cheekbones and large, wide eyes. Had to be their escort. One of her hands rested on the automatic rifle across her lap. The other held a sweating can of cola. She sipped and appraised the s'teeners with an unflinching gaze.

"Afternoon, ma'am," said D'Shay. "We're new colonists." She stared at him. He shifted his feet. "Uh ... ma'am. Do you speak English?"

"I speak English. And WorldSpeak—as you should now. I also speak Swahili, and of course my native tongue, Chewan." She looked at the doll in D'Shay's hand.

"Eh, brown mzungu boy," she said to D'Shay. "You been to witch doctor so you can make a baby? Ha ha."

He laid the doll on a table. "A woman ... dropped it. I thought it was real."

She shook her head. "Woman carry doll for luck to make baby. Also be good comfort—they pretend baby real, like little girl with doll."

"That's so sad," said one of the s'teener girls.

The woman shrugged. "It be God's will."

Jaym frowned. "God wouldn't—"

D'Shay elbowed him quiet.

"So, what do you colony peoples want from me?"

"Nobody met us at the train," said D'Shay. "We don't know where to report."

The woman's face hardened. "You be SUN blenders, yes? Come do many wonderful things for us."

Jaym spoke up. "Ma'am, we're only doing what the Alliance tells us to do. We just need to find some SUN officials to get us to our assignments."

"You not find many SUN peoples. Most SUN jobs be source-out to GlobeTran. But no need for worry, young blenders. SUN, or GlobeTran, office be with government buildings. You go there and somebody assist you."

D'Shay rubbed his pavement-skinned elbow. "How do we find it?"

She took another sip of cola. "You see white government buildings from you train?"

Jaym nodded. "Just past the stadium."

"Go to building with dry waterfall fountain. Globe-Tran peoples be on first level."

"Thanks," said D'Shay, shifting his pack. "Have a *bon dia*, sergeant."

"I be lieutenant," said the woman. She stared at the

group for a moment, looking from one person to the next. "It is wise for each of you to be cautious in city."

"We grew up in cities," said D'Shay. "Rules are likely the same. No eye contact, pair up, watch each other's backs."

She drained her soda and stood. "Yes, all that. Cities have common dangers, but maybe you must discover new rules here. If you do, young colony peoples, some of you may live many, many years."

SIDETRACKED

(Coded message)

To: GlobeTran, Mizambu
From: Alliance Hdqrs. Africa, Harare.

Raiders in the heart of the Highlands are still attacking peacekeeping vehicles. Despite daily airborne reconnaissance, the base of these raiders has not been detected. We suggest that armored personnel carriers accompany all traffic into the Highland area.

————

Two hundred kilometers east of Wananelu, Reya Delacruz watched the passing countryside in awe as she bumped across the Mizambu highlands, the lone passenger in a rusting A-T halftrack. She and her driver had begun the journey in parched foothills outside Bonique City, but by noon the rig had pushed into this woodland that grew thick, green, and sparkled in dew. Now they splashed through puddles in the dirt road from a recent shower.

They drove past towering trees and house-high shrubs heavy with purple blossoms. "Oh my God," she said to the mute driver. "It's ... incredible!" He flicked his cigarette out the window and tapped the steering wheel to the beat of Afro-Pop booming from the speakers.

"It's as emerald as Oz."

The driver lit another cigarette and began to fight the wheel as the A-T whined and slurried up the muddy road. They passed logging camps that all looked the same— each a handful of wood shacks on skids to be dragged to new stands of timber. Many now deserted, some fire-gutted. Looked like war and disease had even punched deep into these forest highlands. A flock of bright birds darted through a clearing like a rainbow of hope. She tried to smile, to think of what lay ahead.

Her holo-card didn't give much information about her blending match. Just his stats: two meters tall, age 22. His name was given as B. Lambaja, but no occupation was listed. But with all these trees he might be a logger. Yeah, a logger. Since he was tall, he'd probably be broad shouldered with a powerful jaw and flashing white teeth. Her lumberjack would swing his ax with muscles that gleamed ebony in the African sun. They'd live in a cabin on the edge of the woods and she'd grow a garden that fluttered with huge butterflies. Parrots would flash through tall trees. Each day her man would return from work to sweep her off her feet and carry her laughing into their log home.

But now the birds and butterflies had vanished. Just a deepening gloom of forest canopy and the muddy road. And so much mud. Rust- and shit-colored mud furrowed by log trucks.

The A-T slewed to a sudden stop. Reya's elbow slammed the dash. "Jesus!" she shouted. "What the hell—"

The driver's face contorted in terror.

Reya looked ahead to see a forest-green Crawler blocking the road. Two Africans in shorts and tee shirts hoisted submachine guns as they walked toward them. Her driver ground gears as he struggled with the floor shift.

One of the armed men fired a burst above the cab. Reya screamed. The driver raised his shaking arms. One man walked to Reya's side of the A-T. She fumbled to lock the door, but he raised his gun and shouted, "No, girl. You get out." He yanked the door open. *"Out!"*

She hesitated until he pointed the weapon at her. Reya stumbled out and stood with her fists clamped, body shaking.

The African looked her up and down. "You be a colony girl, yes?"

"When the Alliance finds out about—"

"Shut you mouth." He pulled out his com-cam. "Smile for birdie," he said, clicking images. He hit 'send' then waited. In a moment he said, "Yes, Bossman. Be colony girl. I think be payment for what I owe, yes? Good. 'Bout one hour." He pocketed the device. "Back in truck, girl."

Reya licked her lips and climbed back inside. The driver still sat petrified, hands in the air. The other man jerked open his door and dragged the whimpering driver to the roadside. Afro-Pop continued to thump. A burst of gunfire flung the driver into a muddy ditch.

Reya screamed. She saw the driver's body shudder as

the smoke of gunpowder drifted through the cab. The shooter climbed into the driver's seat. He laid the rifle across his thighs and fired up the engine. "If you wanna live, keep you hands in lap like good girl." He forced the gears into low and pulled the A-T around the Crawler.

Oh God oh God, she thought. *They're going to rape and kill me. I know they are. If I try to jump, the guy in the Crawler will shoot me. Okay, breathe slow. Gonna get through this.*

She dared a side-glance. He was a small, powerful man with a narrow face. Neck thick as a bull's. She couldn't see eyes behind his mirrored sunglasses. Still the music throbbed. Should she talk to him? Would he beat her if she opened her mouth? She had to ask. "Wh—where are you taking me?"

He took a drag of cigarette. "To you new home, mzungu girl." He looked at her thighs and grinned.

Reya tugged the hem of her shorts toward her knees. "Please... I don't—"

"Quiet. Listen to music. I do not like woman talk so much."

She sat silent, numb, shivering with electric fear. The Crawler veered onto a narrow side road, little more than tire tracks through wet ferns and dense forest. A shower spattered the windshield, quickly turning to a pounding rain. She had never seen so much rain. It drummed on the cab like falling gravel. The crawler slewed up the hill, its wipers struggling on full.

Minutes later he pulled off at a logging camp like all

the others—huts on skids, a few old trailers, but this had a newer building that sprouted half a dozen antennas and dishes.

By now the rain had eased to a steady shower.

The driver honked, then grinned at Reya. "This be you stop, colony girl. Get out."

She looked at the sea of mud outside the truck. Her voice cracked. "Please."

"Do not make you bossman wait. Out!"

She grabbed her backpack and stepped into the rain. Her boots sank into muddy ooze.

Gears snarled and the crawler lurched away. She stood dazed in the ankle-deep muck as rain plastered her hair. Mascara streaked dark tears.

She caught the stench of the place. Like rotted compost and sewage. Shivering, she squinted through rain curtain at the row of shacks and trailers surrounding the mud plaza.

"Girl!" boomed a voice. She turned to see a white man leaning against his trailer door—a pea-green trailer gnawed by rust.

He stood under an awning and sucked on the stub of a cigar. "Over 'ere, girl. Get inside and dry out."

The man's voice was even, commanding. His English carried just a hint of an accent. She gripped her pack against her chest, but couldn't move her feet.

Other figures appeared at doors of trailers and shacks. Mostly black men, a couple of whites. Arms crossed, or leaning against doorways, they watched silently.

Her boots sucked mud as she turned to look at the wall of dark forest behind her.

"Don't even think about it, my dear," said the man, his voice amused. "You've had your look around, now come here." When she didn't move, he snapped, "Get over here now!"

Oh, Sweet Mother of God. Be with me at this moment of my—

"*Now*, Goddamn it!"

She slogged toward the trailer. The shower had faded to a drizzle. Muddy earth steamed as a slash of sun cut across camp. She looked up at his face. Bony angles with a cheek scar that drew his lip to a permanent sneer. He wore only camo shorts. From the gray chest hair and line-furrowed face, she guessed he was in his forties. His eyes were a cold, washed-out blue. He flipped his cigar stub into the mud. "Welcome to Camp-23 and its many amenities. *Mi casa es su casa.*"

Reya shivered at the ice in his voice. She panted her words, voice rising. "He...killed the driver and...kidnapped me. The Alliance and SUN will find me and you're—"

She saw the blur of his fist, but couldn't move fast enough. She splayed in the mud. Her ears buzzed, the side of her face numb. The iron tang of blood ran in her mouth. She coughed and spat.

The man leaned toward her, speaking slow and flat. "I shall only say this once. Camp-23 is my kingdom and I am its god. As god, I'm going to teach you two of my commandments. First Commandment: girls speak only when spoken to. And when you do speak, call me 'Sir.' Second Commandment: backtalk shall cause suffering." He cocked his head. "Now, girl—repeat these two simple commandments."

Reya wiped her mouth, rose to her hands and knees. "I s-speak only when you say to."

"You forgot something."

"Sir."

"Good, good. Now the second commandment."

"Don't backtalk … Sir."

"Excellent." He grabbed her arm and jerked her to her feet.

"My goodness," he said. "You're shaking. No, no, no. There's little for you to fear in my kingdom. Not under my protection."

His gaze slid to her neck and shoulders—to her breasts. She moved an arm across her rain-soaked tee shirt.

"Ripe Mexican fruit." He glanced at the men watching from doorways and chuckled. "The boys look envious. Come, join me in my quarters." He pulled her through the doorway. "Oh, yes—Commandment Number Three: Work before pleasure. You know, '*Arbeit macht frei,*' and all that. Your current task is to prepare my meal. I'm afraid it's leftovers. Heat them up." He pointed to a propane camp stove. A cockroach the size of her thumb foraged beneath the burners.

With a shaking hand she struck a match. The propane flames licked the pot of beans and rice. She wanted to scream, but stood stiff, stirring. Behind her the man lit a cigarette and hissed open a beer. From the corner of her eye she saw him slouched at the dinette table, looking her up and down.

"What's your name, my dear? No, no—let me guess. Maria. Most of you are Marias, no?"

Her back tightened. He had to be looking at her wet shorts, judging her ass. Answer him. Just answer the bastard. "My name is ... Reya."

He flicked ashes from his cigarette and waved a finger. "Tsk, tsk. You forgot something."

"Reya ... Sir."

"Much better. To you, that is my name. 'Sir.' Nothing else. You may hear the men refer to me as Bossman, or Mzungu Boss. I prefer their Mzungu address. It reminds them of my Caucasian DNA. Mzungu connotes the proper mix of respect and admiration." He sipped his beer. "And where are you from, Maria-Reya?"

"Modesto ... Sir. In MexiCal."

"MexiCal. It is a wasteland, is it not?"

She nodded. "We immigrated north."

"Ah. Then you had to be a camp girl. What the NorthAms call 'gees. Or even better, dusties. My, my. I'd say you are quite lucky to be here with me, correct?"

"Yes ... Sir."

"Modesto," he said. "That must mean, 'modest.' Are you a modest dustie girl?" He chuckled. "We shall see."

She clutched the countertop and tried to slow her breath. *Hail Mary Full of Grace. Be with me in my hour of need.*

BEGGARMAN

Urban skills: Avoid city crowds unless accompanied
by a native speaker. Use common sense and the
skills you acquired during your training. In most
settings Blenders will only be seen as curiosities,
but individuals should remain alert.

—*Blender Handbook, p. 37*

Outside the depot, D'Shay spotted the government
buildings wavering in the distance. He turned to
Jaym and the six other s'teeners. "A bunch of us is gonna
attract a lot of attention. We'll break into pairs and head
toward the Alliance building, but let's separate pairs by
half a block. Jaym and I'll go first."

The others nodded, then he and Jaym headed down
the bustling street. D'Shay glanced back. Good, the others were playing it right—acting like they took this route
every day. Avoiding eye contact, walking with confidence.

They passed vendors chanting praises of their goods,
women haggling over yams and oranges, a few blind beggars, feral street kids, and clusters of uniformed school-
children. D'Shay saw a ragged street boy watching a pretty

schoolgirl chatting with her girlfriend. Huh, he thought. Just like the Corridor. The take-it-for-granted wealth, the ignored poverty.

Jaym elbowed him. "Keep walking, but check out the graffiti to the right. The SUN logo." The wall looked pretty much the same as any in the Corridor—the usual tagging and initials—but there was one spray job of the SUN logo—the blue field filled with a yellow sun. But it had been impaled by a graffitied dagger. Drops of red dripped from the blade's tip. Jaym shivered.

"Seems somebody doesn't like SUN, Jaymo." D'Shay turned to the others behind and motioned them forward. He nodded to the graffiti. "If anybody asks, we're Alliance contract workers reporting to GlobeTran. Don't say a word about SUN."

"There's another one," said Jaym, nodding to a wall. "But look at the blade." Stenciled across the dagger was a parade of green elephants that seemed to neutralize the menace of the blade. No words or letters, just the troop of elephants, trunks raised high in triumph. "Any idea what those elephants mean?"

"Not a clue," said D'Shay.

Two blocks later they were walking through a market square. From the crowds of shoppers and vendors a man dressed only in faded cutoffs staggered toward them. Jaym tried to sidestep, but the African's muscled shoulder slammed him.

"Keep moving," said D'Shay. "He's looking for trouble"

Jaym tried to dodge past, but the grinning man shuffled like a soccer player, staying in his face.

D'Shay stepped between them. The man's breath reeked of cigarettes and stale wine. "Hey, ease off. We're not looking for a fight, so how about letting my friend—" An elbow to the jaw knocked D'Shay flat. The man laughed and circled Jaym, his voice rising.

Some in the crowd kicked at D'Shay. As he lay stunned, a man dragged him behind the spectators and started to dig through his pockets.

The red-eyed drunk circled Jaym. "Ehhh, mzungu!" He circled Jaym, leering. Grinning spectators crowded around the pair like schoolboys hoping for a fight.

D'Shay came out of his daze long enough to knock away the man going through his pockets. He shook his head and got to his hands and knees. He tried to focus, struggle to his feet, but someone from the crowd kicked him in the ribs. When the guy tried a second kick, D'Shay grabbed his foot with both hands and snapped his ankle. The man screamed and hobbled away.

D'Shay shouldered through the crowd. The drunk still danced around Jaym, jerking like a puppet to stay in his face.

"Eh, eh! *Mzungu!*" he shouted at Jaym.

Jaym made good moves, twisting, faking, dodging, but the guy leapt like a cat to clutch Jaym's wrist. "*Ndifuna kwatcha. Kwatcha!*"

Jaym grimaced. "I don't have anything. You're gonna break my..."

D'Shay stepped out to grab the drunk's shoulder when the crowd fell silent. People moved aside.

The beggar released Jaym and staggered back as the spectators stared at a robed figure. No, not robes. More like strips of dirty cloth or bandages. A walking mummy.

The mummy man rasped to Jaym, "Ho, moonface. Bet you have kwatchas for old chief Tuntufyie."

Jaym licked his lips. "They ... didn't give us any when—"

The mummy spat and turned to the remaining spectators. "Kwatchas for old chief?" People scattered.

D'Shay grabbed Jaym's arm and they bolted away.

BACK STREETS

Assignments in large cities at first can be
disorienting. If you become lost or sense danger,
simply locate a helpful Alliance or GlobeTran guard
on patrol. They will be happy to give directions or
escort you to a place of safety.

—*Blender Handbook, p. 43*

---

amn, thought Jaym. What the hell happened back
there? We get the shakedown by a street bum, and the
crowd turns into a pack of jackals. Not one person helped.
Only that raggedy ghost that appeared from nowhere broke
things up. Not something the *Handbook* prepared us for.

Jaym and D'Shay now found themselves dead-ended
in a deserted square. Jaym glanced behind them. "Hey,
what happened to the other blenders?"

D'Shay shook his head. "Probably took off when the
crowd got rowdy. But the gov buildings can't be far. Look—
I'll try that alley to the left. You scout the other side."

"Fine, but stay within shouting distance. I don't like
the feel of this place. Especially after our interaction with
the locals. Meet you back here in ten minutes."

Jaym carefully moved down the alley that forked and twisted in a maze. Some branches ended in box canyons sealed by building rubble or bullet-pocked walls. But he finally found a narrow passage that seemed to cut through to the direction of the government buildings. He whistled for D'Shay and they took off together.

By the time they reached the gov building with the dry waterfall, the sun was low, shadows deep. Jaym read the lettering over the double doors.

ALLIANCE & SUN HEADQUARTERS,
CHEWENA BRANCH
Administered by GlobeTran, International.

The windows were shuttered and dark. Jaym rattled the locked doors. "Damn!" He glanced around the plaza. Across the street a few lanterns glowed from shops. Tinny pop music rolled from a bar.

Of the handful of people lingering in the plaza, most were GlobeTran guards strolling their rounds. One, a stocky African woman, walked toward them, rifle slung muzzle-down. Her voice grated like sandpaper. "'Ey. You be colony boys, yes? What you doing out after curfew?"

Jaym tried not to stare at her weapon. "Our train got in late...ma'am. And the Alliance office is closed."

She shook her head. "Is too, too foolish to be out in nighttime. Did they teach you nothing in your fine Blending school?" The woman held out her hand and snapped her fingers. "Show ID."

They handed her their tags. The woman scanned them by streetlight, then squinted at their faces. "You," she said to D'Shay. "This photo does not look so much like you."

"Yeah. Bad lighting, and the lens must have—"

"Silence!" She read the data codes. "Give you name and birthtown."

"Well—sure, ma'am. But, hey—you don't think—"

Jesus, thought Jaym. *Don't mess with her, D'Shay.*

"*Quickly!*" she said, flipping her rifle's safety latch.

He raised his hands. "Hey, hey. Name's D'Shay Green. Born in NorthAm, Corridor Sector, Annex 12."

She held the tags in front of D'Shay's nose before she let them clatter to his feet. "Blenders, colonists. You gonna save Africa, eh?"

"We're just going where SUN tells us," said D'Shay. "Maybe you—"

"Drop it!" whispered Jaym.

"Go 'way," said the woman. "Get to holding compound. I see you more tonight, you be arrested."

"Holding compound?" said Jaym.

She shook her head. "You colony boys know nothing." She jutted her chin toward a narrow street across the plaza. "Go there. Take you south to river. Look for camp tents. *Go!*" She turned and strode away.

D'Shay picked up their tags.

"Real sweetheart," muttered Jaym. He glanced at the narrow street snaking into darkness. "Suppose she's sending us into gangland?"

"Loosen up, Jaymo. That GlobeTran sweetie may not

be Miss Personality, but she did give us directions. Come on. I'll bet the street's gonna be full of kitty cats and grandmas handing out cookies."

They trotted down plaza stairs, into the dimly lit street the woman had pointed out. They passed shopkeepers pulling metal grates across storefronts, street vendors packing up carts. Beggars were settling into nighttime doorways while families huddled around small cook fires in alleys. They walked faster to get past the mingled stench of boiled cabbage, burnt meat, and dog shit.

Further on, the streets grew darker. Jaym's neck hair prickled as he looked into shadows, broken out windows. "D'Shay, this is not good. We gotta hole up till morning. Flophouse, empty shop ... anything."

"Ease up, Jaymo. This hood's deserted, and the camp shouldn't be far."

They walked for another twenty minutes, stopping at a dark intersection to get their bearings. Here most shop fronts were boarded over, sidewalks strewn with glass and trash. Across the street a scrawny yellow dog with a torn ear slunk away, eyeing them.

Jaym whispered, "I'd rather take my chances back—"

D'Shay waved him quiet. "Listen."

Jaym held his breath. There. Somewhere ahead. A pattering. Footsteps running this way.

"Move!" said D'Shay, jerking Jaym into a doorway. Within seconds shadows jogged toward them. They pressed against a doorway, as a half dozen panting shadows exploded past. Excited voices. Bare feet slapping paving stones. When the footsteps faded, D'Shay said, "What was *that* about?"

"Dunno," said Jaym, "but we're dusted if we hang around here."

They tried to retrace their path, crunching glass underfoot as they moved through the coal-blackness of deserted streets. D'Shay kept trying locked and gated doors as they moved down the street. "Hey!" he said to Jaym. "Over here. This one's unlocked."

They crept inside and shut the makeshift plywood door behind them. A slight glow of starlight from a ceiling window allowed them to see silhouettes of two large chairs. "I'll be damned. A barbershop!" said Jaym.

The seat cushions had been torn off the chairs and tossed on the floor. D'Shay kicked the dusty cushions together. "There. Two mattresses."

"Good enough for me," said Jaym. "Now, gimme a hand with one of these chairs. I want the door barricaded for the night." Together they wrestled one of the iron chairs across the floorboards and against the flimsy door.

Within a few minutes D'Shay was snoring softly. Jaym lay on his lumpy mattress, wide-eyed and listening intently. He heard rats skittering inside the walls. Outside the distant singsong wail of a siren sliced the night.

Another sound. Voices? Yes, and the patter of running feet. Then a shout. "No! Please . . . don't—"

A scream. Excited African voices. So close. Shit! Had to be just down the street. Jaym shook D'Shay.

"Wha—?" he mumbled.

The patter of running feet again. Laughter and chatter in another language.

"They chased down someone. A blender, I think. He screamed, not far away."

They listened. Dead quiet now.

"Don't even think about going out there now," said D'Shay.

"But what if the guy's hurt? Maybe wounded badly?"

D'Shay lay quiet for a moment. "Gangs like that don't leave somebody wounded."

MAI-LIN

That first night after being abducted, Reya lay in the
dark, curled like a fetus at the foot of Bossman's
bed. She shuddered, her sobs muffled in the wadded sheet,
her body aching from his drunken blows. The screech of
a forest monkey made her heart pound. It was a cry too
much like the winds that shrieked when dunes had begun
to rise around her MexiCal home.

From the dim moonlight glowing through tattered
curtains, she could see the dark form of Bossman sprawled
across the stained and stale sheets, a bloodstained cloth
wrapped around his hand.

At first he had laughed at her struggles, but when she
kneed him he beat her nearly senseless. She worked her

tongue against a lower incisor loosened by his fist. But biting his hand to the bone had been worth it. If only he had knocked her out cold she wouldn't have had to feel him, smell him. God. How had Mom endured Remington? She edged away from the hairy leg that twitched in drunken sleep.

Yesterday afternoon, while cleaning up after the bean mess of a supper, she discovered a dull butcher knife under the sink. But even if she could force herself do it, what if he screamed? Guards would cut her down before she made it to the trees.

She was trapped, maybe for the rest of her life—which might be very short with these thugs. And Plan-B was now hopeless. No way could she contact Jaym or D'Shay now. Would they discover that she never made it to her assignment? And she doubted that the SUN or Alliance cavalry could even try a rescue in this dangerous land-of-the-lost.

A tapping on the trailer door made her jerk up straight. With her heart pounding, Reya held her breath and slowly stood, pulling the sheet tight around her. Bossman muttered in his sleep and rolled over. The tapping again; more insistent. The door handle rattled.

"Boss's woman," whispered a soft voice. A girl's voice. Reya unlocked and cracked open the door. A small figure stood in soft lantern glow. At first glance she looked like a child. An oval Asian face with hair cropped in a severe pageboy. But the girl's eyes were older. Maybe a s'teener, like herself.

"I am Mai-Lin," whispered the girl. "Be dressed. I take you to work job."

Reya noticed the girl's critical gaze. Appraising her bruises, her matted hair, her ear piercings. *Go ahead and judge me*, thought Reya. *Just get me away from here.*

"One minute," Reya whispered. Inside she pulled on rain-damp clothes and slipped into muddy boots. She stepped outside and gently closed the door. "I'm Reya," she said.

Mai-Lin made a slight bow from the waist. In the lantern light Reya tried to read the stony expression of this girl.

Reya followed Mai-Lin across the camp. "What is this place?" she asked, searching Mai-Lin's face.

"This no place. Not on map. But we talk about this later. Now we make morning meal for men. I am glad for you to assist. Job too big for one girl."

She followed Mai-Lin around the field of mud toward a wide woodshed on log runners. Nearby, the parked Crawler loomed in the lantern light. Reya stopped, nodded at the crawler. "They shot the driver. Killed him for nothing."

"They not kill you if you not fight them."

"But he didn't fight."

Mai-Lin shrugged and walked on. "Come. We make our work."

Inside the mess hall, Mai-Lin flared her lantern and set it on a plank table. "Men eat here," she said. In the kitchen she lit another lantern and hung it over the stove. "We cook so big strong men can raid and steal. Must make food for thirteen." She rummaged through cupboards to heft out pots and kettles. "You build cook fire, Rey-ya. Wood by stove." She handed Reya an apron.

"Fire? But we have solar. I saw the—"

"They use solar for their 'flectors and Com center. We get leftover for water heater, but we need fire for big cooking."

Reya put on the apron and turned to the rough-built stove of welded steel plates, maybe scrap torched from the hulk of a burnt-out tank or APV. She fumbled newspaper and kindling through the stove door. She'd seen her uncle do this when they fled north through the hills of northern MexiCal. He had to use pages from the family Bible and pieces of bark. Like he had done, she wadded paper surrounded by a wigwam of small sticks. She struck a match, and gently blew on the struggling flame. The kindling took fire.

"Good," said Mai-Lin. "Build fire big and hot." She lifted the iron kettle to the stovetop. "Must boil much water."

Reya added kindling, a split log, then closed the stove door. "Mai-Lin, how long have you been here?"

"Almost three month."

"You from China?"

"Yes. Farm in Hunan. One year at university before Canton Plague. Family all dead."

"Sorry," said Reya.

When the water began to boil Mai-Lin scooped cups

of cornmeal and flour from tins and tossed them into the bubbling kettle.

"What's your... 'man' like, Mai-Lin? How does he treat you?"

Mai-Lin stared at the stove, her lips puckered. "It not wise to talk about such things. Best to work, not to think, Rey-ya. You cannot survive here if you think ahead, or behind."

Maybe she was right. Work and sweat might numb her fear. Ease her nerves.

"This how to make coffee," said Mai-Lin. Into another kettle of water she tossed handfuls of stuff that looked like ground bark mixed with dirt and leaves. They lifted bowls and cups from the cupboards while the water came to a boil. When Reya dipped out a cup of coffee she scalded her tongue on the first bitter sip.

Mai-Lin threw handfuls of eye-burning peppers and chunks of dried fish into the mush while Reya churned the yellow-brown muck with a wooden spoon the size of base-ball bat. A monster cockroach scurried across the stove. Reya held her breath, snatched it up. It hissed, twisted, and bit her thumb before she flung it in the gruel and stirred it down.

Mai-Lin smiled.

"A little protein for Bossman," said Reya.

After ten minutes of stirring, Reya's wrists ached. "This done yet?" she asked.

Mai-Lin stood on a stool to look into the kettle. She nodded. "Yes. It ready for men."

The door banged open and several Africans swaggered in. Reya's heart leaped. Oh God. Would he be with them? Would he brag to the others about last night?

More men clomped through the doors, laughing. Reya wiped at the counter, eyes down. "'Eh, lookah. The new colony girl," shouted one. "Eh, new girl. You give Boss-man good ride last night?" More laughter. She clenched her jaw and stirred mush. Her ears buzzed and the room whirled. She grabbed the counter. *Have to get through this*, she thought. *Just through this moment, then the next...* She steadied herself and stood erect. Her eyes blazed as men poured coffee and headed to the long tables.

"Oooo," said another voice. "Lookah her face. She mad. She be fighter girl. Hey, colony girl—you a fighter? You make Boss a good fight? Ha ha."

"Don't talk to them," whispered Mai-Lin. "Give them food. And don't look at eyes. They not like girl to look at their eyes."

With shaking hands Reya ladled bowlfuls of the fishy porridge, then carried the trays to the tables.

"Looka Boss girl's eye," said one. "It puff like turtle eye. What you do for that one, feisty gal? Look like Boss get tiger girl, eh? You tiger woo-man? Ha ha."

She set a bowl before each man. *Dear Mother of God, give me the strength to bear this morning.*

"You gimme little sugar too? Ha ha."

Please. Just this morning.

More men banged through the door.

Reya heard his voice. Her knees nearly gave way.

Images of last night roiled like choking smoke. She swallowed. No eye contact. Don't say anything. Can't throw up now. Just keep walking toward the kitchen.

"Had a good look at my new girl, boys? Don't look too hard. She's my property." He sat at a table with two other whites. Reya noticed the blood-spotted bandage on his hand. Several of the Africans glanced at the bandage. Bossman held up his hand. "Dog bite. Any questions?" The men looked at their bowls and spooned mush in silence.

Reya stumbled into the kitchen and knocked over a stool. Mai-Lin touched her arm. "You okay?"

"I...I can't face him."

"Give me tray," said Mai-Lin. "Fill more bowls for when other men come. I serve."

Reya nodded, wiped her eyes with shaking hands. "Thank you, Mai-Lin. God, I'm sorry."

"You be okay. Make slow breath." She patted Reya's arm. She hoisted the tray of bowls and headed to the tables.

Reya filled more bowls. She watched from the kitchen. My God, she thought, Mai-Lin was taking such a chance.

"Hey, China girl!" growled Bossman. "I want to be served by my Aztec princess."

"She little sick, Bossman. Might throw up." She kept her eyes down and placed steaming bowls before him and the other white man.

Bossman's fist clamped Mai-Lin's wrist. "Get her out here, China bitch." Mai-Lin gasped. Her face paled, but she looked down, silent.

Reya squeezed her eyes shut. *Dear God, please don't let him hurt her.*

From another table, a stocky African with thick arms stood. His voice echoed even and cold. "Eh, Mzungu Boss! China girl be mine. Not even you hurt her."

Bossman's face burned red. The mess hall fell silent. For several heartbeats no one moved. Finally the boss slapped the table, laughed, and shoved Mai-Lin away. "Pah. I'm not hurting your little Chink. But teach her to respect her betters."

The men laughed nervously.

Mai-Lin hurried to the kitchen. She cradled her wrist, tried to smile at Reya. "It okay," she whispered. "He not hurt me."

———

Later, when the men had left in their trucks and Crawlers, Reya and Mai-Lin stood at the sink, scrubbing bowls and spoons.

"I owe you big time," said Reya.

"Camp women must help each other. It is how we survive."

Reya rinsed a stack of bowls. "Your man stopped the boss. He must care for you."

Mai-Lin shrugged. "He protect his property. Nothing more. He take chance with Bossman because he head African man here. Must save face before others." Mai-Lin glanced around, then whispered. "You must be very careful, Rey-ya. Your Bossman have wild and killing eyes.

Sometimes when man like that get drunk or jealous, they kill woman and nobody care."

"Why hasn't the Alliance taken this camp out? One drone would wipe it out in a second."

Mai-Lin rubbed her wrist. "Camp has shields and 'flectors. Alliance drones see nothing, so the men raid and kill and nobody knows where they come from."

"No chance of a rescue for us, is there?" said Reya.

Mai-Lin shook her head. "Can only rescue ourself."

RETURN OF
THE MUMMY

HANSEN'S DISEASE is characterized by disfiguring skin sores, nerve damage, and progressive debilitation. It was hoped the disease would be eradicated in Africa in the 2050s, but the Pan-Af Wars intervened.

—*African Diseases (SUN Pamphlet #12)*

Near dawn, D'Shay and Jaym eased open the shop door and cautiously stepped into the empty street. The sun had not yet risen and the corridor of broken-down shops was a shadowy canyon. In the dimness they found the body, face up in the middle of the cobbled street. Jaym knelt beside the dead boy. He stared at the surprised death mask of a blond s'teener, a blender like them. The boy's throat was slashed, jaw agape. Flies were already clustering at open flesh.

"Damn!" said D'Shay. "I remember him. This guy was with us. He took off with the others when that drunk beggar cornered us."

"His ear," said Jaym. "It's cut off."

"Both are gone," said D'Shay. "Damn. We're outta here."

As they stumbled through deep-shadowed back alleys, Jaym kept listening for the sound of those street voices from last night. Eager, deadly voices. He tried to shake the image of the s'teener's blood-drained face. The vacant eyes staring at the African sky. Jaym knew if they turned the wrong corner, they might be facing a street gang ready to open their throats as well. "Hey," said D'Shay. He pointed ahead.

"What?"

"I remember passing by this caved-in brick building. It was maybe only a klick in from the main street we were on yesterday. We're outta here, Jaymster!"

"Heh heh!"

They froze.

"Eh, colony boys! Heh, heh." The voice came from a shadowed doorway to the right.

"Don't mess with us, man," said D'Shay. "We got knives."

"White boy," said the shadow voice. "Even though I almost blind, I see you pretty good. Heh heh. That be 'cause you mzungu face shine like moon."

Jaym took a step back.

"I'm warning you!" said D'Shay.

The heap of rags swayed from the doorway and shuffled toward them. Jaym could smell the man's rotted flesh. "You! You broke up the street crowd back in the square."

"Yes, we meet again, Moon Face. Heh heh. I be old Tuntufyie. Tuntufyie the beggar." He pulled raspy breaths. "Before Death Years, Tuntufyie be big man in his village. Be headman then." He shuffled toward Jaym.

"What do you want?" asked D'Shay. "Money? Sorry, but we're busted." He tried to make out the man's features, but his face was a dark well. Mummy rags surrounding a black hole.

"Heh heh. You think Tuntufyie be a thief?"

"No," said D'Shay. "But, hey—we're just passin' through. Trying to find our people."

"Who be you people now? I think you have no people. Heh heh. You colony boys be like leaves blowin' across field. You small boats lost in great sea." The raggy man turned to Jaym. "You give something for old Tuntufyie?" His stubby fingers clamped Jaym's wrist. "Gift for a chief?" For an instant Jaym caught a glimpse of face—the cavern of a nose, a glint of an eye.

He tried to jerk his arm free, but the old man's grip was fierce. "We don't have anything. We just came—"

"Hear me, Moon Face! If I not help, you gonna die soon. Bad boys cut you open like melon and take you ears. But Old Tuntufyie can show you to the safe place for colony boys. Yes. Yes I can. I not be greedy, but I think you must give something nice for Tuntufyie to save you lifes." The old man coughed a laugh. "What be worth you life, Moon Boy? Maybe much fine tobacco?"

"We've got a few Alliance coupons for food," said Jaym.

"We'll give you those." *God*, he thought, *was leprosy contagious?*

"Not 'nough!" snapped Mummyman. "You lifes only worth 'lliance paper?"

Jaym considered the fifty SUN ration notes hidden in his boot. But that money was his lifeline for train tickets and bribes.

"Give us a break," said D'Shay. "That's all we've got."

"Tuntufyie sick of colony boy games. I whistle for bad boys if you not gimme something 'portant, quick quick."

"Okay," said Jaym. "Lemme check my pack." He rummaged. "I've got rations and a bag of Choc-o-Mints. I'll bet you'd—"

Tuntufyie spat. "You insult me, Moon Boy. Time for street boys to bleed you and take ears. I watch them butcher you like chicken."

Damn. No choice. Jaym kneeled to untie his money boot.

"No boots," said the old man. "Not interested."

"But I'm—"

Tuntufyie stepped toward D'Shay. "What that shine on you wrist, brown mzungu? Be gold?"

D'Shay sighed, then pulled off the watch. Tuntufyie squinted at it in the faint lighting. "Tell time?" He held it to his ear.

D'Shay nodded. "It tells time great and the dials glow in the dark. Even is self-winding. No batteries needed. But this watch is worth a lot more than—"

Tuntufyie turned to Jaym. "Choc-o candy too, then

you follow Tuntufyie. Do not walk like buffalos. You kick trash can and street boys come bleed you fast. Heh heh." Jaym followed his whispered footsteps, D'Shay on his heels. Twice the beggar paused, listening, then moved ahead.

Two blocks further Tuntufyie froze. Jaym crouched. Holding his breath, he peered into darkness, listening. There! Voices drifting from the street ahead.

Tuntufyie motioned. "Behind trash cans. Lay flat like lizards."

Jaym and D'Shay dropped to the pavement, scrambling behind the cans, squirming tight against the brick wall. Broken glass bit into Jaym's thighs. His cheek pressed against something, sticky, rotted. He choked back barf and wormed back from the rot. His foot struck a sack of garbage. A bottle rattled across the alley. He clenched his fists. *Shit oh shit!*

Footsteps ran toward them. "*Ndisiyeni!*" shouted Tuntufyie. "*Nditana apolisi!*"

"*Moni, Tuntu. Muli bwanji?*"

Through a thin gap between trash cans Jaym could see four of them. The leader in front casually swung a rusted machete at his side. The others held meter-long iron pipes. Damn!

He and D'Shay lay flat, trying to breathe slowly, silently. Through the centimeter crack Jaym saw the leader—a coal black teen with a shaved head—shook his fist and shouted in Chewan. Tuntufyie held up his rag-wrapped hands. "*Iai!*"

Was it a plea? Tuntufyie waved an arm, pointing in the direction of the rising sun.

The gang leader's voice was a monotone of menace as he tapped the ragged man's chest with the tip of his machete. Tuntufyie spoke in a soothing voice as he gently pushed the blade away. The leader snorted, lowering the machete.

"Pitani bwino!" said Tuntufyie as the gang trotted in the direction he had pointed.

When the footsteps faded, the old man laughed softly. "You colony boys be good lizards—'cept lizards not kick bottle 'cross alley."

Jaym stood, his entire body shaking. He wiped the rot from his cheek, then retched and splattered the sidewalk.

"Heh, heh," said the ragged man. "The police make a big, big fine for that, Moon Boy. Heh, heh."

"Why they after ears?" asked D'Shay.

"'Gade men pay ten credits for pair of white ears. You worth ten silver credits, Moon Boy." He turned to D'Shay. "You ears, brown mzungu, worth nothing. Could be any city boy."

"But I send them on duck chase to old empty part of city to find you. Heh heh." Tuntufyie looked down the alleyway. "Come."

Jaym stayed close to Tuntufyie's silhouette as the old man crept through alley shadows. Within minutes they were approaching a main street with bicyclists and pedestrians on the sidewalk. "You be safe now, colony boys." The old man paused. "When you get to you blender village, you tell peoples 'bout Tuntufyie. Tell how he be big city chief. How he save you lifes."

"We will ... Chief," said Jaym.

"Now go! Go to right, look for cook fires."

"Tuntufyie," said Jaym, "what do ...?" He looked into the alley shadows, but the old man had vanished.

WELCOME CENTER

Flitt-Trans memo: Bonique Processing Camp to Alliance Hdqrs, Harare.

Two NorthAm Blenders arrived 0615 today. Assignment cards seem valid, but arrival time suspicious. Please run check on Blenders NA-2678 and NA-2891. Will hold both until clearance received.

The processing camp looked like an abandoned park, now fenced by a three-meter-high fence, entirely choked by some kind ofAfrican ivy. The entrance was a wire gate topped with loops of razor wire. A sign on the fence read:

WELCOME CENTER FOR NEW ARRIVALS.
TRESPASSERS WILL BE SHOT.

"Sends kind of a mixed message," said D'Shay.

The guardhouse behind the gate was an unpainted plywood shack. Jaym shouted, "Anybody there? We're incoming blenders."

There was muttering from the shack, and finally a skinny African stepped out rubbing his eyes. He wore only a GlobeTran cap and plaid boxer shorts. "What you blender boys doing here one day late? Others all come yesterday when they supposed to. And why you be here this time of morning?" He glanced at the sun, just rising above steaming rooftops. "Come back in two hours. I'm not on duty yet. Need sleep."

"Hey, no," said D'Shay. "Please let us in now … sir. We almost got our throats cut by street gangs. We just wanna get behind the fence. Okay?"

The man muttered something in Chewan and wandered back into his shed. He returned with a ring of keys. "You lucky I be a good guard. Maybe you can find little something for this good guard—before I let you go to assignment." He grinned.

Jaym nodded. "Thanks, we'll come up with something." *Geez,* he thought. *Did everyone over here think blenders are flush with money?*

The gate creaked open and they stepped inside. "Thanks, man," said D'Shay.

"Go to back of last tent row and do not bother more."

"Oh, hey," said Jaym. "One last thing, please."

The guard sighed. "What!"

"Did a girl with light-brown skin and black hair come in yesterday?"

The guard shrugged. "Blenders look same to me. 'Cept this one," he said, nodding toward D'Shay.

"She had big hoop earrings," said Jaym, fingering a circle by his earlobe.

The guard frowned. "Yes, the earrings. I 'member now. I told her not to go to assignment with ear gold. Too easy for thief to grab and tear her ear."

"Is she here?" asked D'Shay. "Her name is Reya. She's a friend."

"No, she be picked up by lorry driver yesterday. Gone to assignment village. That what you get for coming late!" The guard locked the gate and started into his shack. "No more talk. Just leave me to sleep. Go!"

They wandered between rows of flimsy tents—maybe a couple of hundred. Most were empty. A few were still occupied by sleeping blenders. Jaym didn't recognize any faces. "Looks like most came through and shipped out right away," he said. "Wonder how long we'll have to wait?"

"Dunno," said D'Shay, "but let's catch some shut-eye. Not much sleep last night."

The last row was all empty tents. Jaym threw his sleeping pad into one and flopped down. He was out in seconds.

———

Jaym's two weeks in processing camp seemed like two months. The daily routine: eat stale rations; play cards; lotion his sun-broiled hide. God, how had Reya survived 'gee camp for two years? Reya would be deep into her assignment by now. Man, he'd sure like one of her kick-ass pep talks to settle his nerves today.

Jaym suspected he and D'Shay had their ship-out dates delayed this long because they had pissed off the guard. They never did cough up a bribe. Okay with Jaym. He was in no great hurry to get dropped off at some remote village.

He glanced at his escort schedule: *Wananelu train station, 0800 Tuesday.*

D'Shay crawled from his tent, yawned, and stretched. "So, it's Day Zero for you, Jaymo. Hey, tell me the name of your village again."

"Nis ... Nish-wa ..."

D'Shay looked at Jaym's assignment form. "*Nswibe.*" C'mon—that's not so hard to say. Don't forget that we gotta set up for Reya's Plan-B. When I get a free day I'll get out to *Nswibe* and we can touch base. While I'm there you and your lady can show me the hot spots."

Jaym forced a grin. "Me and the missus will be watchin' for ya."

D'Shay chuckled. "Praise the Lord that I got assigned to the Big City. I'm allergic to pythons and other jungle shit."

Jaym shifted his pack. "Well, can't make my escort wait."

"You take care, man," said D'Shay.

"You too." They rapped knuckles, then Jaym turned and walked out the gate.

NSWIBE

Nswibe: Chewan village, 13.57 S; 33.41 E.
Population unknown. May have become deserted
after the Pox swept that region of Chewena in
2049.

—*Global Alliance Gazetteer, p. 583*

Jaym followed the train tracks two klicks east to the whitewashed depot where a half-dozen African men held hand-lettered signs. There: *Mz. Jaymm JoHAsoN*. The old African cradling the sign stood bony and withered.

"*Buon Dia.* I am Jaym Johansen."

The man gave him a jack-o'-lantern smile and nodded. He wore a hole-riddled tee shirt beneath his frayed sport coat. Stork legs thrust from his shorts like polished ebony. His splayed and leathered feet were dyed rusty red from road dust.

Jaym offered his hand. The man stared at it, then reached out with a handshake light as a girl's. "I be name Bzono," he said with gap-toothed good will, a light in his eyes. "Come, mzungu. I take to Chewena wife."

Wife! Jaym's heart raced. *Geez, not yet. What if she hates me at first sight? And what if she's a witch? Or maybe the family will—*

Bzono held out his hand. "See you paper."

He stared numbly at Bzono. *Wife.*

The old man gently slid the assignment paper from his fingers. He squinted at the words and nodded. "Yes. Good village. I think you wife be in 'portant family. Come, mzungu."

Bzono walked from the platform. Jaym snapped from his daze and trotted after him. Even though Bzono was a head shorter, the African stretched out his ostrich legs and moved quickly ahead.

Within an hour they were on an old highway heading into open country. Low, rolling hills lay brown with brush and sparse trees harboring flocks of thick-billed birds. The asphalt road had now turned to gravel and dirt.

They came across sooted hulks of burnt-out trucks and tanks, bomb craters, makeshift graveyards. At one, a woman was digging a hole for a shoebox coffin. All around her, tiny graves were decorated with plastic windmills and homemade dolls.

Women still trying for a miracle.

They passed barefoot boys, and girls in faded dresses or wraparounds. He ignored their stares. Sunburned pale-faces had to be a rare sighting.

By late afternoon, he sucked the last drop of water from his canteen. His legs wobbled, feet throbbed. Bzono steered off the road to take a skimpy trail that wound through low hills. The path was little more than a goat track through grass, brush, and struggling trees.

Jaym spotted a few com-poles—primitive wood poles with wires dangling. Useless now, but any infrastructure was hopeful.

Soon they veered onto a smaller trail where he staggered behind Bzono to a ridge top. A shallow valley lay before them. On the far side, wooded hills rose into low clouds. He heard the distant whisper of falling water.

At first he didn't notice the village tucked in brush and trees. His heart dropped at the sight of a dingy cluster of adobe huts with thatched roofs, fifty or more. The place looked like something from the Stone Age.

Bzono must have read his expression. "It not what you think, young mzungu. That be old Nswibe Village. Pock kill much." He waved at the huts. "Old Village dead now. Must stay away. Bad spirits live inside."

Jaym nodded. Reya had told him how Monkey Pox-III had burned like a crown-fire through parts of Africa with an 80 percent fatality rate. The epidemic had raged two years before they found a vaccine.

Bzono detoured him around the old village. There were maybe fifty or sixty homes. Some were simple wood structures, others adobe with faded paint. It was like a ghost town, as if people just got up one day and left. A corn grinder stood unused, a rusted and spider-webbed bicycle leaned against the wall of one house. And, God, there was a pull-toy—a little wooden lion on a string, just sitting by a doorway. Was there a child's skeleton lying in bed in that house? As they passed, a few mangy chickens scurried in and out of the ghost homes. The warm breeze rustled the remnants of grass roofs. It carried scents of mildew, dust, and death. Goosebumps tingled up Jaym's arms.

Beyond the spirit village a tethered goat munched on grass stubble. Jaym had never seen a real goat. Never smelled its sharp musk. The animal's elfin eyes followed him. He sensed the judgmental gaze of the goat, as if it were a disapproving sentinel. Maybe a sign of what he was about to encounter.

Half a klick further lay a circle of two dozen small adobe homes in a cluster of green trees. "That the new Nswibe," said Bzono. As they neared, the old man pointed to a tiny house painted sky blue. "I think that be you family."

"But, you said important."

"'Portant not always big." He waved a hand. "Now, you go, mzungu."

Jaym shifted his pack, legs wobbly.

"Come." Bzono took his arm and gently tugged him toward the open door. He spoke softly in Chewan, soothing as a grandfather.

The scent of cool earth and spices wafted from the interior. Bzono leaned forward to speak quick, soft words. In a moment a slender man with flecks of gray in his wooly hair stepped out. He glanced at Jaym and Bzono, then touched a forefinger to his lips, a hush. Bzono returned the gesture. A little girl and boy slipped behind the man. The children also did the finger-to-lips greeting, wide eyes fixed on Jaym.

He copied the gesture, then Bzono spoke in sing-song, throat-clicking Chewan. He tapped Jaym on the chest. "Mzungu Jay-em," said the guide. He gestured toward the older man. "Mistah Eduard Zingali."

Mister Zingali stared at Jaym with steady sun-red eyes. No smile. He handed Bzono a few coins and said something in Chewan.

Bzono made a slight bow. "I go now, Mzungu Jay-em. Good-bye."

Mr. Zingali motioned to the open door. "Lowane, Mzungu Jay-em."

Jaym watched Bzono disappear down the trail, then looked to the cobalt sky. The curve of a single hawk tilted on an updraft. Free to fly anywhere.

He turned to Mister Zingali, then ducked into the dim interior. Jaym stood rigid, nails dug into his palms. Small windows let in leaf-filtered light. He glanced around the room, trying to resolve shadow shapes.

He made out a woman in a chair and five girls, pre-teens and teens, sitting against the far wall. Too dim to see their features, but he sensed gazes moving over him. Appraising. Still no one spoke. Mr. Zingali squatted on his heels. Should he squat too?

Finally, the seated woman spoke in a high sing-song voice. He could see her hair, too, was flecked with gray. Had to be the mom.

Mr. Zingali touched his elbow, "Seat, mzungu. She say for you to seat."

"You speak English!"

"Only little."

He shrugged off his pack and heel-squatted like Mr. Zingali. But after a long minute of silence, his ankles wobbled and he knew he would tip on his butt. He plopped cross-legged on the mat, graceful as a buffalo. One of the younger girls giggled before she could clap her hands over her mouth. The older woman fired a string of harsh words at her.

He tried to make out faces of the family shadowed and silent against the wall. There were two older girls. His blending match had to be one of them.

Mr. Zingali looked to the girls and nodded. One hesitantly moved forward. She walked over to kneel near her father. Her fists were squeezed tight, her lips pinched.

"This be Lingana," said Mr. Zingali.

Jaym's heart hammered as the girl looked up with large, dark eyes. She looked beyond him, her chin high. Oh God, he thought. That aloof gaze. Already his first test of being a blender was being squashed by this girl. He wondered what happened to rejected blenders. He looked at the door. If he only had the guts to bolt and run.

But ... to where?

ONE PERCENT

To: GlobeTran, Inc., Mizambu
From: Global Alliance, Harare.

Continue drone reconnaissance mission over Miz Highlands for one more week. If no results by then, shift operation to next quadrant south until further notice.

Copy: Global Alliance World Headquarters, Geneva.

Reya was into Week Two at the camp. Once again she lay in the dark, huddled in bed while Bossman snored. Groggy from constant lack of sleep, she watched for dawn to touch the trailer window. She slid off the sheets, quietly dressed, and waited for Mai-Lin. Finally came the familiar tap at the door.

Outside she twisted her hair in a knot as they walked through the steamy morning, heavy with the scent of moldering leaves and mud. Hovering ground fog glowed orange in rising sunlight.

"Face look better, Rey-ya. Not so puffy."

"I don't struggle anymore." She hugged herself, her voice wavering. "God, Mai-Lin. I've become a whore."

"No! You *not* a whore, Rey-ya. If you a whore, then I whore too. We just women who survive. It not like this forever. Someday it better."

Reya stepped over fresh dog turds. "Mai-Lin...is it a sin in your religion to want to die?"

Mai-Lin stopped, gripped Reya's sleeve and looked fiercely into her eyes. "Sin is to give up. We strong women. Must *never* give up."

"They caged me in the 'gee camp, and now I'm trapped here with a brutal asshole. No more. I'm...gonna try to get out, even if it's only a one-percent chance. I'd rather die trying than be caged like this."

Mai-Lin said softly, "Maybe can make more than one percent. We talk later, after morning work. Wait till men 'way from camp."

Yeah, she thought—later. Mai-Lin seemed so accepting of all the crap of this place—the demeaning BS of the men, the ten-hour days of sweat in kitchen heat, and being as trapped as 'gees back in the Corridor.

"Now we go cook," said Mai-Lin. "No more talk."

Reya bit her lip until she tasted blood. If she didn't, she'd lose it and scream out her rage. She wiped her eyes, nodded, then followed Mai-Lin.

————

They took their time during morning cleanup, waiting for the last truck to leave camp. "It safe to talk now," said Mai-Lin.

They carried steaming coffee cups to a mess table. Reya stirred sugar into her cup and glanced at the ceiling. "What if we're being bugged?"

"I check good. Nothing here 'cept spider and roach bugs. Besides, we only stupid girls."

Reya smiled. "Right. I forgot. Okay, I'll throw out a plan for starters. We gather supplies, then we find a way to poison or drug them so we can slip into the forest. We'll find a forest village and get a ride to—"

Mai-Lin waved her silent. "No killer herbs 'round here. We find roots to make strong drug, but these big men. Root drug only good for few hours. We not even certain it can work on all the men. If it does not, then they send wolf dogs after us. Other women have tried to escape in past, but dogs find them fast. Eat them." She tapped her chewed-down nails on the tabletop.

They sat for a minute. Reya absent-mindedly finger-traced an eye-shaped knot in the wood tabletop. So, even if the men were drugged, they only had a short window of time to get clear of this place. Drugs alone wouldn't work. Somehow the men would have to be killed. Sure, they could get knives, but the chance of killing them all at once was about one percent. If one of the men cried out, the women would be gunned down in a minute. Her fingers hesitated at the eye-shaped knot. *Ohmygod! That's it!*

"Eyes!" she said excitedly. We'd be taking a big chance, but I think I know how we might pull this off!"

———

They worked through the afternoon, cooking, cleaning. When all had left the mess hall, Reya and Mai-Lin worked out the details of Reya's idea.

But they talked for too long.

Reya hurried back to the trailer as the setting sun threw slanted shadows across the camp. Bossman sat on the steps, waiting. He dangled a beer bottle between two fingers, swinging it like a pendulum, his eyes slits, his face unreadable.

He stood and walked toward her. "Where have you been?"

She took a step back. "The water heater. It broke so we had—"

"Bullshit! You've been letting *kaffirs* poke you after hours, haven't you!"

Reya forced a nervous laugh. "Boss, don't be ridiculous. We just—"

He drove his fist into her gut. She folded in the dirt, gasping for air.

"Bitch. Trying to make a fool of me? You know I could cut your throat and nobody would say a word. The dogs would enjoy fresh meat."

Sooty balloons of pain floated before her face. Mouth gaping, she fought for a breath of air.

"You will not make a fool of me!" Bossman cocked his head and laughed. "You look like a fish in the bottom of a boat." He turned and strode toward the camp tavern.

She got to her hands and knees before she vomited. When her breath returned she stood and leaned against the trailer. She wiped mud and barf from her cheek. In her haze of pain she replayed Mai-Lin's words:

We strong women. Can never give up.

At the sink she rinsed mud and vomit from her face. "I am *not* your woman," she hissed between clamped teeth. She looked in the cracked mirror and lifted her chin. "I am *not* your whore. I am Reya Barbara Catherina Delacruz. I am loved. Mom and my sister love me. The Virgin Mother loves me."

She opened the kitchen drawer and drew her thumb across the blade of the butcher knife she had honed razor sharp.

INQUISITION

Using SUN's socio-psychological profiles, we have
selected a life partner who will be a compatible
spouse. If at first there is discomfort with your
Blender match, time and necessity will heal
any perceived difficulties. (See Appendix 32 for
relationship issues.)

—*Blender Handbook, chapter 3, "Your New Partner"*

L ingana turned to her parents and spoke rapidly. The
only word Jaym recognized was *mzungu.* "White
man."

As she talked he stole a glance at her body. Long neck,
slender arms. Small breasts and nipples pressed against her
flower-patterned tee shirt. He looked further at her narrow
waist. Slim hips and thighs in loose tan shorts. Dark legs
tapered to bare feet. He looked back at Lingana's face. A
nice face. Small nose, large eyes, long lashes, full lips, and a
high forehead. Like other Chewan women and girls he had
seen, her hair was cropped close to her head.

He looked back at her eyes. She was now staring at his

nose, her eyes wide. Was there something on his nose? She saw him looking and glanced away.

In the back of the room, the younger kids squirmed and poked at each other. They had to be older than eight. Pre-Flare children. The mother snapped at them and the room fell silent.

All eyes turned toward him, waiting. The moment he'd been dreading—speech time. *Okay, just do it.* He cleared his throat. "I'm very glad to be in your ... home."

Blank expressions.

Crap—now what do I do? He cleared his throat. "I don't speak your language, but I can talk WorldSpeak.'"

The mother glared and waved the children out the door. She then fired a string of Chewan at Lingana.

"My mother has worries," said Lingana.

He raised his brows. "You speak English?"

She frowned. "Of course. I took five years of English in school."

"I didn't mean to ... uh, sorry."

She paused, giving him a look. Disgust? Puzzlement? He couldn't read her. Finally she nodded toward her mother. "Mother does not speak English or WorldSpeak, only Chewan. She is the head of our clan and keeps the old ways. Only Chewan for her."

Jaym looked at the mother, still giving him the evil eye. "She seems piss—angry with me."

"She had hope for a brown mzungu. She worries our children will be pale with frey-kill spots and long noses."

Our children! His face heated. His voice cracked.

"Okay, maybe some freckles. Noses probably won't be as flat as—I mean, not that yours..."

Shit.

She translated to her mother who gave him the evil eye.

Mr. Zingali said something to his wife and Lingana. The women nodded, but looked back at Jaym as they stepped outside.

Mr. Zingali stared at Jaym for a long moment. Jaym squirmed. What now?

"Our talk not be for women. I ask questions, man to man."

An inquisition? He kept an even expression as he said, "Yessir. Ask me anything."

"You know you bring big danger to our village, yes?"

"Me? But I..." Jaym's thoughts whirled. I'm no danger. The only dangers they warned us about were urban thugs and a few renegades in the countryside. Wait—maybe this is a way for Mr. Zingali to get rid of this paleface sent to possess his daughter.

Mr. Zingali cocked his head. "Did they not warn you that the 'gade men come lookin' for blender people. They want Africa for selfs. So, when they find blender in village, the village suffer much." He paused, locking eyes with Jaym. "But blender suffer more."

Jaym licked his dry lips. "Have... the 'gades come here?"

"Not yet, but have burned villages near. Killed blenders."

Oh God. He tried to keep his voice steady. "So ... what should I do? Keep out of sight?"

Mr. Zingali shook his head. "No. Must live lives and trust God. We need you blenders to make babies. Must chance danger for better future. We do our best to keep you and village safe. We watch for 'gade people. Try to hide you if they come."

Try? Damn. Will they really "try?" Mr. Zingali might, but what if someone hands me over to the 'gades to save their own skin?

"Now," said Mr. Zingali, "do you believe in Jesus?"

"Jesus?" *Oh no. Are we going born-again here?* "Uh, sure. Jesus was a great man. Maybe the greatest."

"Then swear on Jesus you tell me truth."

"I swear ... on Jesus."

"Then I make two questions. One: Do you beat woman?"

"Geez, no sir."

The old man scanned his face, held Jaym's eyes with his. "That be good, 'cause our people do not allow men to beat woman. It be a great punishment to beat woman. We make clan trials for offenders. But if you beat Lingana, I not wait for trial." His eyes flashed. "And if I am gone, Giambo—her older brother—will make justice."

Jaym swallowed, but kept his eyes on Mr. Zingali's. "I promise, sir. I would never hit a woman."

He nodded. "I see in eyes you speak true."

"Thank you."

"Question two," said the old man.

Jaym straightened his back. "Yessir."

"Do you fornicate?"

What is he asking? Do I sleep around? Read dirty mags? Masturbate x-number of times a day? What did this have to do with anything? Maybe it was something Biblical, like the Old Testament stuff about shepherd boys getting off with their sheep. Or maybe "fornicate" had a totally different meaning in Mr. Zingali's head.

Mr. Zingali frowned. "Why do you wait? Question is simple. Do you fornicate?"

"Sorry, sir ... but 'fornicate' has many meanings where I come from."

"Is simple. Do you sleep with other womans besides you own woman? That be fornicate."

Jaym blushed.

"You face be red. So, you fornicate?"

"My face is red ... because I've never ... I've never had sex with a woman."

Mr. Zingali blinked. "You joke me?"

"I've, um, never had the chance."

Mr. Zingali smiled, then began to chuckle. "Never been with woman! Not even street woman?"

"No sir. Not even a street woman."

"You be with man, then?"

"Oh, no, sir. I'm straight. I mean, I like women. I just—"

"Then you be virgin boy? Hee hee."

Jaym looked down. Face burning.

The old man shook Jaym's arm. "That okay, Mzungu

Jay-em. Better to be virgin than cheater man who fornicate. I just be surprise that 'Merican mzungu not have womans. Men in 'Merican cinema always get womans."

Jaym shrugged. "Those are just stories, sir."

Mr. Zingali nodded. "I believe." He turned to the door and shouted. Lingana and her mother came back inside and knelt near him. Mr. Zingali spoke in rapid Chewan with its clicks and impossible throat gymnastics. At one point the two women jerked their heads toward Jaym. The mother lifted an eyebrow. But Lingana's expression … surprise?

"Do not worry, Mzungu Jay-em." The old man grinned. "Village people not need to know." He motioned to Lingana. "Daughter Lingana speak to you now. She decide or not."

"Decide?" asked Jaym. He glanced at Lingana's penetrating gaze.

"Our people accept blenders," said Mr. Zingali, "but we—Lingana—say 'no' if she not pleased how you make answer."

"But, SUN …" *Just shut up*, he told himself. *I'm going to dig a deeper hole if I keep talking.*

Lingana's parents moved near the back wall and sat on low stools. Lingana sat on her heels a meter from Jaym. She was quiet, studying his features, searching his eyes.

After a long minute, his face burned. He glanced away from her piercing eyes, looking past her. He focused on the low kitchen table and its sturdy, brightly painted stools. His eyes drifted to the pots and pans hung on the wall.

On the far wall he made out the faded photo of an African couple.

He glanced back at her eyes. Still she was silent, watching him. *Damn! why doesn't she get it over with?*

He turned to feign a cough. For the first time he noticed their household shrine. Just a small table in a corner with a flickering candle and two figurines—wooden heads of an African man and woman, beautifully carved and polished in ebony. On the wall above hung a gold-leaf cross with a black Jesus.

Lingana's voice broke the silence. "Why do you stare at our shrine? Are you judging our beliefs?"

He cleared his throat. "No, no. I'm just … curious. Only looking around."

"Yes, but it is the *way* you look at things. Do you think we are primitive people?"

"Hey, that's not—"

"No, we do not live in lush flats, and, yes, we respect many of the old ways—like having a house shrine."

He looked at her flashing eyes.

"Look, Lingana. Do you know what culture shock is?"

"I think so. Means to be anxious in a different culture, yes?"

"Exactly. Well, I'm *fried* from my culture shock here in Africa." He tried to keep his voice level. "So please don't judge me too quickly. I'm trying not to judge you or your culture." He looked down. How could you not judge this place? Here he was in a dinky, primitive village and a bare-bones little house with its voodoo shrine.

Still avoiding her eyes, he nodded to the shrine. "What kind of shrine is it?"

She hesitated. "My parents follow the old gods, but we include Jesus since I go to Methodist services in the city. The shrine is a blending of beliefs."

A blending, he thought. What irony.

"Do you go to church?" she asked. "Or do you believe in nothing?"

"I don't go to church now because we don't have many churches left. We had riots. Religious nuts—zealots, crazy people—bombed churches they didn't like. I used to sneak into an old ruined church to look at the colored windows that weren't broken. Sometimes I'd sit and wait for something religious, but ... I never felt God there."

Lingana spoke softly. "Have you never sensed God?"

Was this the rejection-or-not question? He hesitated, then said, "I did feel something when were coming to Africa. It gave me the shivers."

She cocked her head, waiting.

"On the ocean. On the deck of the ship all you could see was water. Seemed like the whole planet was water. Huge waves and storms that tossed our ship like a twig. I knew kilometers of dark water and undersea mountains were below. It gave me kind of a scary feeling. But a feeling of some big connection too. I really can't describe it."

"Like God?" asked Lingana.

"A raw power ... maybe God."

Her face softened. "I think I understand. I feel God in

church, but also in the forest—even the song of a sunbird can—"

Mrs. Zingali spit a question at Lingana. Lingana turned and calmly said a few words. The mother nodded, but frowned at Jaym.

"What was that about?" Jaym asked.

"Mother is impatient. She wants to know your answers. I told her you believe in God. That is important for her. Now I ask a very different question."

He nodded.

"How can I be certain you will be a good husband and father?"

Jaym shifted his butt on the hard floor and puffed his cheeks. "That's a tough question." *Crap*, he thought. *This is like a job interview for something you know absolutely nothing about. I could BS, but she looks too bright. She'd nail me.*

"How can you not know?" she said. "You must have thought about this. Are you trying to avoid the question?"

Jaym spread his hands. "Look, Lignany—"

"My name is *Lingana!*"

"Sorry…Lingana. But my dad wasn't much of a husband or a father. He ran away when I was a kid. I only hope I can do the things he didn't."

"Will you work hard as other men?"

"I'm a good worker. I have training to help your village too."

She stood and spoke to her father in Chewan.

Jaym glanced at her slim back, tiny waist, and gentle flair of hips.

"Lingana be done with question, for now," said Mr. Zingali. "Mzungu Jay-em, SUN choose you special to work for our village, yes?"

"Yessir. SUN and the Alliance."

"What they train you to do for our village?"

"Um, hydro … sir."

Mr. Zingali's expression was blank.

"A 'hydro' is someone who helps houses and villages get water. Plans water pipes, wells, and irrigation."

He frowned. "But we have strong wells. Much water. Pipes good."

The room was silent. *Damn. So his hydro skills meant nothing here. Okay, he had to take another tack.* He straightened his shoulders and tried to sound convincing. "I'm also trained in solar. If your village needs—"

"Solar?" interrupted Mr. Zingali. The man's face brightened. "Yes, yes. Our village needs solar fixed!"

Lingana translated to her mother. The mother nodded. Her face uncrimped a little.

"Village solar station be broken," said Mr. Zingali. "Has not work for many years. You fix it?"

Jaym suppressed a smile. *Yes! At last he'd get to use his solar skills. He'd be SolarMan, village hero.* He waited a beat, then said, "I will do my best."

"Good, good. We talk of these things later. For now it best for you to move into house of oldest son, Giambo."

Lingana and her father exchanged a glance. She avoided Jaym's eyes. "My brother … is not home yet. Giambo does his work now. He will come for the evening meal."

Her father stood. "I take you to Giambo's house. You sleep there. Keep you things there, for now." He paused. "I tell him to behave good."

Jaym tried to read Lingana's expression, but she looked away, staring at the little shrine.

HOUSECALLS

"If we do not change our direction, we are likely to end up where we are headed."

—*Chinese proverb*

———————————

When the camp men went on their daily raiding missions, Mai-Lin began to pay visits to their women. Although Chinese New Year had passed two months ago, she announced that it was this week and carried a tray of rice cookies and a pot of tea from house to house. She did this with great caution—sipping tea, letting the women talk, and gently edging the conversation to the real topic.

Zetta Cristobal whooped when Mai-Lin finally revealed the plan she and Reya had devised. "'Bout damn time some girl got brave 'nough for this. What do you want me to do? I can shoot a gun. Drive a lorry, or I—"

Mai-Lin's eyes brightened. "You drive?"

Zetta nodded furiously. "I worked on ostrich ranch when a girl. Before wars I drove lorries to market. I am a good shot too. Kill many hyenas."

"Can you drive Crawler?"

"Lorry, Crawler all the same. Gears gonna be different, but I don't sweat."

Mai-Lin approached Flora Andula with greater caution. A tall, regal woman, Flora bore tribal scars like chevrons on her cheeks. Camp rumor said she had been a village shaman before being taken. Flora rarely smiled or mixed with the other women.

Mai-Lin found Flora out back taking laundry from the line. Flora looked at the plate of rice cookies. "What do you want?" she said unsmiling, tossing undershirts in a basket.

"It is Chinese New Year. Cookies are big tradition."

Flora unpinned a sheet and folded it. "I see you making many visits in camp." She put her fists and on her hips and glared down at Mai-Lin. "What do you really want?"

"You tell me first. What do you want, Flora? What you do want most of all?"

Flora glanced behind her and hoisted the basket onto her head. "Come. We better talk inside."

———

Reya timed the flyovers of the Alliance skimmer. It droned near camp about noon, and evenings around 1800 hours. Sometimes men stepped outside to watch the skimmer, laughing as it passed blindly overhead. From what she could pick up from their conversations, the drone probably carried enough air-to-ground missiles to pulverize the camp in a single pass.

It was after dinner and Reya and Mai-Lin scrubbed burnt pots and greasy frying pans. They had the mess hall to themselves.

Reya's arms were up to her elbows in oily suds. "You heard any talk, Mai-Lin? Any days that might work?"

"I think Friday. My man been bragging 'bout big raid. If it has success, I think they celebrate hard."

"Then let's go for it," said Reya. "You sure the other women will do their parts? If it doesn't work..."

"Yes. If it does not work we may all die. But every girl is willing. I trust all. Even tavern girls."

"Everyone's gotta act normal. We keep to our routines. Can't get even one man suspicious."

Mai-Lin nodded. "I tell all women they must continue as humble servant. No one smile."

———

Friday, late afternoon.

Bossman and the others skidded into camp with whoops and bursts of skyward gunfire. The camp women watched from their windows.

Bossman jumped from his Rover and shouted from the camp plaza. "All women, front and center! Now!"

Reya, Mai-Lin, and the others cracked open the doors of trailers and wooden shacks. Women hurried to the plaza, faces anxious.

"Let's have smiles, ladies. It's been a fine day. Time for your men to celebrate. Fetch the good whiskey—my private stock—and a case of Cape Town beer from the tavern. While you're there, bring back both silicon maidens. You cooks there, get your arses in the kitchen and concoct a feast to honor this occasion. Roast a damn pig or something. Get moving!" More shooting and whooping from the men. They lit cigars and swaggered toward the mess hall.

Zetta Cristobal clapped her hands and shouted. "Come, girls. We must honor our brave men with best food and drink." Zetta pointed at three women. "You, you, and you. Fast, fast to tavern for much drink. Bring tavern girls and boss's best whiskey." The three nodded and trotted toward the camp tavern. Zetta turned to Mai-Lin and whispered, "That antelope meat still be good?"

"It some bad, but enough peppers and curry they not know."

"We'll get started on the meat," said Reya. "Come on Mai-Lin."

Inside the mess hall, the men gathered around a table struck by sunlight from a window. Bossman sat as the others stood to watch him open a black velvet cloth and spread it on the table. In the sunlight, the gems glittered in rainbow hues.

"Looka those beauties," said one man. "Many, many carats."

Bossman lifted a stone to a shaft of light. "Notice the color, boys. Pale blue and flawless."

Mai-Lin fired the stove while Reya diced the tainted antelope haunch. "What'd the men get?" asked Reya.

"Diamond stones. Look like they catch big-time dealer."

Three women banged through the screen door lugging a case of beer and bottles of whiskey. The two tavern girls sauntered in, swishing their hips and carrying open bottles of scotch. "You private stock, Bossman," smiled one. "I pour for you?" She leaned over to allow a generous view of breasts barely covered by her sheer slip.

"Keep your pants on, boys!" shouted Bossman, "This one's mine tonight." He held out his glass. "To the brim, my dear."

She filled the glass. "Share with other men, Boss?"

"Today only. I'm feeling generous."

"Who be thirsty?" asked the girl. Her gold-flecked eyelids lowered and she cocked her hip.

Men pressed forward with water tumblers. "Me first," one yelled. "No, me. I be a leadman," shouted another.

"Shut up!" snapped Bossman. "Let the ladies do their work. And no groping while they pour. I don't want any spilled whiskey. This is your only taste of my stock, gents. And no drinking until I make a goddamn toast!" Bossman raised his glass. "A toast: To the driver of the armored car who followed our 'detour' sign. And to the guard who shat his drawers when he ran. May they both rest in peace."

Laughter.

"Drink up, boys." He drained half his glass.

As they drank and laughed, one man reached for a diamond glittering on the velvet.

Thunk! Bossman's knife bit into the table top, impaling the webbing of the man's thumb.

He yelped. "I just want to touch!"

Bossman jerked the knife free. "I do the touching. *Comprende?*"

The men stood silent. The one with the bleeding hand grit his teeth and wrapped a dirty kerchief around the wound.

"Enough of that," said Bossman. He emptied his glass. "Let the celebration continue." He shouted toward the kitchen. "For Christ's sake, hurry with that food. We've spent a hard day at work." The men laughed.

Mai-Lin, Zetta, and Reya sizzled yams and chunks of gray antelope meat in garlic and pepper sauce. By the time they carried out trays of food, many of the men were moving in slow motion, their voices slurred. Some sat alone, talking and chuckling to themselves. At one table, men arm-wrestled. Bossman watched the wrestlers strain. Their elbows slid, and one man crashed to the floor. "Pah. You boys are soft as girls." He took another bite of antelope and pushed away his plate.

Reya whispered to Mai-Lin. "Zetta said they'd all be out by now."

Mai-Lin shook her head. "Not yet. They big men." The tavern women watched from a corner. One nodded to Reya.

Thump! Another man slumped to the floor. Bossman staggered over and toed him in the ribs. "Humph. I've never seen my men get this drunk. It's like—" He held the bottle to the light. Swaying, he turned to Reya and Mai-Lin, his eyes wide. "The whiskey! God damn!" He snorted a laugh. "You bitches doped the whiskey! I'm going to gut each and every one of you." He fumbled to unsheathe his hunting knife.

Mai-Lin ran to him and bowed, staring at his feet. "No, Bossman. Old whiskey stock is the very highest proof, even for strong men. Look! See, you are fine 'cause you are strong."

Bossman brushed her aside. He hesitated, swaying. "Yeah, that's why I'm Bossman." He grinned, then shouted, "Back to the kitchen, slant!" He stumbled toward the tavern women. "I get you both. We're…" He reached for a table, but spun and crashed to the floor. He lay face up, eyes wide, confused. He mumbled. "I'm…Boss…"

Zetta walked to his side. "Big Bossman not even match for taste of scorpion root? Shame, shame. Time for you to have nice, nice sleep."

"Lemme help," said Reya. Ribs cracked when she stomped the heel of her boot on his chest. He moved his lips but only drooled.

Only two men remained upright, propped by their chairs. In moments, one slid to the floorboards. The other's head dropped back, mouth agape and snoring.

"Good job!" Mai-Lin said to Zetta.

Zetta nodded. "Used 'nough root to knock down herd of rhinos."

Reya booted Bossman again. "Okay, ladies, time for Act Two."

TINMAN

Since the destruction during the Pan-African Wars of 2051–52, few Chewan industries have managed to revive. Most commodities, such as furniture, pottery, and metalware, are created in each city or village in small workshops.

—*Blender Handbook, chapter 26, "Chewena"*

D'Shay elbowed up on his sleeping pad. His dream involving twin redheads evaporated all too quickly. He squinted around the room. Yup, still stuck in Monsta-Girl's house in Wananelu.

His tongue smacked of moss from last night's dinner. Not much variation in Chewan cuisine. Mostly spiced-up yellow paste—gunk in a bowl. Sometimes they tossed in dried fish, other times meat. He spooned one chunk last night with fur still attached. Roadkill?

He rubbed chin stubble and surveyed the cramped living room—the only place the family had to put him. His couch-bed was made from a packing crate padded with faded paisley cushions. Across the room were two wooden chairs, and a flamingo-pink table supporting a goldfish bowl. A goldfish in Africa? That big lake they passed on the train had to be full of flashy tropical fish, yet here swims a limp goldfish. He walked over to the bowl and tapped the glass. "Hey, buddy. Be of good cheer. We'll make it."

A young voice bubbled from the kitchen. D'Shay quickly put on cutoffs, tee shirt, and sandals. He trotted through the tiny kitchen, making an awkward grin to the toothless grandma and the girl trying to spoon mush past the old lady's gums. Both watched him hurry out the back door to the neighborhood outhouse—a timeshare toilet.

He hurried in, held his breath, and let it stream. And stream. He zipped up, burst outside, and gulped fresh air. D'Shay looked at the hazed blue sky. Another blistering day. It had been hot during Corridor summers, but here the sun seared you. Broiled your skin. And it'd only been two weeks. Fourteen days down and the rest of his life to go.

At first he'd been relieved to be assigned to a city. He didn't want anything to do with mucking cow shit or chasing chickens. But this wasn't the city life he bargained for.

He trudged back to the kitchen.

"Morning, D'Shay," said the girl. "Time for morning meal." The little girl was a welcome bright spot in his new life. Big smile, wide eyes, and wearing a calico dress from some African Goodwill. She took care of Grandma, cooked, and always had a ready grin. Trapped as tight as Goldie, but somehow cheerful.

"Morning, Chirilie." He pulled up a chair and watched her feed Grandma. The withered old woman stared at him like she knew him from some past life.

"Mornin', Gramma," he said with a wink. The old gal made a slight smile, a spark in her faded eyes as mush dribbled down her chin.

Chirilie slopped a ladle of yellow-gray paste into a wood bowl and pushed it to D'Shay. He lifted an eyebrow. "'Scuse me, waitress. I ordered steak and eggs. Eggs over easy with a dash of Tabasco. I think the chef made a mistake."

Chirilie blinked. "You do not like?"

"Yeah, yeah. Just kidding. You know—a joke. It looks ... great."

He poked at the mush and thought about the day ahead—working with Chirilie's dad and older brothers at their tinware shop. D'Shay's NorthAm training had been carpentry. Basic stuff like framing walls, hanging joists, even some plumbing and electrical. Most houses here were a mix of brick, concrete, and corrugated roofing. Seemed like everybody managed their own shabby carpentry.

Anyway, he could do elementary metalwork with the guys, especially since the family tin shop was low-tech. Each day he and the boys cut, forged, and hammered oil drums and scrap metal into buckets, washtubs, and watering cans. Amazing that they could take a rusty sheet of metal and bang and forge it into a shiny pot or pan that looked like it came off a machine assembly line.

They'd started him out with simple stuff, like heating scrap metal till it glowed red for the boys to work on. Easy enough, but on his first day he couldn't get the tin the ruby-red they wanted. He let it cool to an ashen gray then grabbed it from the coals. It sizzled his thumb to blisters. The guys got a good yuck out of that.

D'Shay spooned down more porridge and watched Chirilie wipe Grandma's chin. Chirilie was a pretty little girl. Slender, smooth chocolate skin, fine features. Why couldn't Philira—her big sister, and his SUN-match—have a little of Chirilie's looks and charm? Philira was half a head taller than him and built like a gorilla. Even had the makings of a mustache. But then, she wasn't exactly excited to see him. When he had showed up on the front porch that first day, she cussed in Chewan, elbowed him aside, and gorilla-stomped from the house.

"She thought you gonna be a mzungu," Chirilie had explained. "But she say you nothin' but a African mzungu."

When big ol' Philira clomped back home that first evening, she looked mean as a pit bull. He hid beside the house till she slammed into her room and started snoring. Praise the Lord for his living room bed.

He put his spoon in the empty bowl and pushed back from the little table. He patted his stomach. "Chirilie, you cook a fine breakfast."

The girl made a sly smile. "You like way I cook you eggs?" she asked.

He kissed his fingertips. "Perfect."

She giggled.

He carried his bowl to the sink. "Hey, Chirilie. How come you're not in school? You on spring break or something?"

"No more school. Since Mother went to heaven, I

must be home to cook and care for Grammy. This be my job now."

He rinsed the bowl and spoon in a pan of tepid water. "How many years of school did you have?"

"I finish grade four. Last year. Father said that be plenty for girl. I know numbers and 'nough English. Can read better than big brothers!"

"Yeah, but you're such a bright girl. You deserve to finish school."

She shrugged. "Who would take care of Grammy? Who would cook and clean? We not be rich 'nough for housekeep woman."

He watched the girl talk to Grammy as she patiently spooned more mush past the withered lips. "Well, if you ever get a chance, go back to school. You're too smart to be a maid forever."

"Thank you DuShay." She looked at him with those big eyes. "Maybe I get chance someday. If I do, I think I become nurse. I like to help people who cannot help selfs."

"Good goal. And Grammy isn't gonna..." *No*, he thought, *don't go there*. Chirilie looked puzzled.

"Oh, darn," he said, grabbing his lunch sack and water bottle. "I'm late for work. So, bye, Grammy, Hi ho, hi ho, it's off to work I go." He paused. "Oh, Chirilie? When's Philira home from work tonight?"

She shrugged. "'Bout six. Maybe seven. She say they have two truckload of chicken to butcher."

He could almost smell the stink of chicken guts Philira carried. "Okay, sweet girl. I'll be a little late myself. Gotta stop off for a soda with the boys and talk about important things." He slipped out the door and into the morning heat.

While walking to work, he passed the market shouts of vendors; the caws of ravens squabbling over gutter scraps. He waved through clouds of flies by butcher stalls and dodged bikes and carts at the square where just weeks ago he and Jaym had been harassed by the drunk, then strode west past Mummyman's alleys.

Hadn't thought of Jaym for a while. He'd be living in sweet paradise in a hillside village with his country babe by now. Each day Jaym would astound the villagers with his hydro and solar work, then get a fine meal and some loving from his chocolate sweetie.

D'Shay wound through the litter of an alley to enter the rear of the family's tin shop. One of Chirilie's older brothers was already pumping the bellows at the forge. Even though two sides of the shop were open to the outside, the place was hot as a corner of hell, with the sun beating on the metal roof and the forge throwing out blasts of superheated air. On one side of the shop lay stacks of rusted barrels, sheets of warped tin salvaged from a ravaged building, and unrecognizable shards of iron. On the other were shining kitchen pots, watering cans, frying pans, and even boxes of newly forged hammers, chisels, and other tools. The floor was dirt, so the place smelled dank and you could almost tasted the tang of solder and metal in the air. "Morning, Chaz," he said to the sweating boy.

He glared. "I be *Gemmit*. You cannot tell yet?"

D'Shay tied on his leather apron. "Sorry, Gemmit. So, where's your clone?"

"Not clown. Twin. We eternal twins and be very different."

"'Fraternal.' But you look like the identical type to me. Unless Chaz has a mole on his butt and you don't."

"You make joke? Charles have big ears and bend nose."

Although Gemmit and Charles had identical noses and the same jug ears, he said, "Yeah, I'm messing with you. You guys really do look different." He glanced around the shop. "So, where are Chaz and Pop?"

"Be at market selling."

D'Shay checked out the pile of flattened tin. "Okay, what's on the assembly line today?"

Gemmit held up a shiny new sprinkling can. "Water cans for village peoples. Same as yesterday. You make metal flat. I bend and solder."

"Can do." D'Shay hefted a flattening hammer. He grabbed a sheet of tin from the corner of the forge.

Sssss.

"Shit!" He ran to the cooling bucket and plunged his hand in the water.

"Ha ha. When you gonna learn use tongs, DuShay?"

"How about a little sympathy?"

"Like you mzungus say, 'No pain, no gain.' Ha ha."

———

At day's end, he and Gemmit helped Pop and Charles unload their cart of unsold watering cans. Pop looked at D'Shay's swollen fingers. "Pretty soon you hands have 'nough scar they be tough like gloves. Ha ha."

"Yeah, ha ha. You folks sure get your laughs outta this, don't ya?"

"Yes," said Charles. "You be funny addition to family. Hee hee."

"Come, boys," said Pop. "We cool off at Red Lion."

Charles grinned. "Bet DuShay wanna hurry to home for Philira. Think she take love bath with much, much perfume soap." The brothers laughed.

"Ho ho," muttered D'Shay.

At the Red Lion, D'Shay got an orange soda from the bar and collapsed at a table with Charles. As always, the tavern's tinny music throbbed with the same ancient disco beat. Gemmit played a game of pool on the tattered felt table, while a row of red-eyed regulars sulked at the bar. D'Shay slid sandals from his aching feet and cooled his seared fingers on the chilled soda bottle. Pop went straight to the bar to flirt with the bartender—a broad-shouldered, chain-smoking woman, who was also the house bouncer. Pop told one of his tired jokes and the woman made a polite chuckle.

"How come you don't drink beer, D'Shay?" asked Charles.

D'Shay sipped his soda. "No offense, man, but the beer this place serves tastes like goat piss. Hard to mess up a bottle of orange soda."

Charles laughed.

"Chaz, can I get serious with you? I mean, can you keep it from Pop and the others?"

Charles leaned close. "Okay. Man to man. I keep quiet."

D'Shay ran a finger around the lip of his bottle. "It's just that...I like you guys—and Pop is a great boss, and Chirilie is a doll. But Philira..."

Charles nodded. "Big problem. Philira mean as Cape buffalo. Just bad luck for you, DuShay."

D'Shay stared at his soda bottle. "Philira's gonna cut my throat some night, I just know it. And she, uh..."

"She be ugly like mudfish," said Charles. "I be a good brother, but she be mean and hard to look at." He took a slug of beer, winced, and wiped his mouth.

D'Shay nodded. "Besides Philira, I know there are guys in town who would like to carve up us blenders."

"Yes, I hear of them. People who work for 'gades. Double bad luck, DuShay." Charles lowered his voice. "You be a good fella for a mzungu, DuShay, but I think you live longer in 'nother place."

D'Shay raised his eyebrows. "Somewhere else in the city?"

Charles shook his head. "Alley boys always hunting for mzungu blenders. You skin not so dark, so they probably take you ears—just in case."

D'Shay recalled the mask of the dead blender in the alley. Throat gaping red, ears bloody stubs. He shivered.

SOLARMAN

Solar film-sheets developed in the early 2060s have allowed some villages to produce electricity with little infrastructure. Many poorer or isolated villages, however, are still dependent upon earlier solar arrays with antiquated equipment.

—*Global Alliance, Africa—Internal Report, June 3, 2067*

———————————

Jaym spent his first night in Nswibe alone in Giambo's hut, a barebones shack on the edge of the village. The place looked to be made of salvaged cargo crates that created walls with a crazy-quilt of words indicating container contents, some in English, some Chinese. Some upside down, some sideways.

He turned up the lantern and walked around the single room. He read some of the English lettering on wallboards:

9MM HOLLOW POINT AMMUNITION, 2000 ROUNDS

THIS SIDE UP

DIAPERS, DISPOSABLE, 1000 PACKETS

Diapers, he thought. That shipment had to be pre-Flare. At least eleven years ago.

Giambo's hut was barely large enough for a cot, a wash-basin, and a rough-hewn table. No chairs. By the door were a tattered pair of dirt-coated running shoes, a few dusty tee shirts and shorts tossed in the corner, and an unwashed plate and fork being raided by tiny ants.

Jaym alternated between pacing the small room and sitting on the cot picking a hangnail bloody. Mr. Zingali had said he didn't know if Giambo was coming home tonight or not. He said sometimes his son disappeared for a day or two.

Jaym figured he could sleep on the dirt floor if he had a blanket or sleeping mat. There was only a wadded sheet and a yellowed pillow on the cot. But if he used the cot and Giambo came home drunk...

He stepped outside and scanned the velvet-black sky. The night was impossibly dark. An hour ago the sunset had lit the hills on fire, but within moments a curtain of night fell and stars shone so bright it was like you could jump and grab a handful.

A meteor traced the sky. He made a hopeless wish.

———

The next morning a little boy shook Jaym awake. He sat up, stiff from the hard floor. He glanced at the cot. No Giambo. The boy handed Jaym a bowl of mush and a spoon, then tore back out the door.

Jaym stood and stretched his aching back. He stepped outside and looked for an outhouse. Nothing. He headed for a clump of bushes and peed. Back inside he spooned down the mush. It tasted like bitter cornmeal, but was warm and filling. Okay, time for a public appearance. He glanced in the cracked wall mirror. The best he could do was finger-comb his hair and splash his face with water from a tin basin on the table. He dressed and stepped into the morning glare.

Mr. Zingali sat in the shade of the next hut, puffing on his pipe. "Mornin' Jay-em."

"Morning, sir."

"You fix our solar now, yes?"

He tried not to show a sudden panic that seized his chest. "Uh, sure ... I can look at the station, but I don't have tools or parts to fix it."

"We find tools for what you need. Come, it be good time to work before gets too hot."

Jaym shivered, recalling the voices of his mother and the Alliance interviewer: His mother's disappointed face as she said, *Oh Jaym, if only you had gone into solar;* The Alliance interviewer's, *Sorry, but your solar scores are too low.*

No. Don't listen to them. Time to erase those messages. This was his chance. He could do it. Had to.

He followed Mr. Zingali into the village square and froze. Ohmygod! Thirty or forty villagers watched him from patches of shade. Even Lingana and the rest of the family were there. As he and Mr. Zingali walked from the village and across a grassy field, the people followed in single file. He didn't glance back, but heard soft voices, children giggling, and the pad of footsteps.

Mr. Zingali stopped at the rusted safety fence. The abandoned solar station stood behind in the thin shade of a gnarled tree. He nodded toward the small building with its tilted tower of collecting panels. "You fix now, yes?"

"I'll see what needs to be done." He dared a glance at the crowd, looking for Lingana. There—she stood holding the hands of her two little sisters. When he caught her eye, she looked down.

Okay, he thought. *Quit thinking about the eyes on my back. Just get to it. Show them what you can do. It's the one way I might gain a little respect—maybe acceptance.*

He scanned the solar setup. Hard to tell how old it was. Vines webbed the tower and panels; frayed wiring dangled loose. At least it hadn't been scavenged for copper. From what he could see here, all he'd need was liquid solder and metal tape to patch the lines. Must be some in the big city.

Next, check the central mast. He kicked through brush to the rusted ladder and climbed the vine-wrapped mast. He avoided the upturned faces below.

The mast panels had been warped by high winds, some scorched by lightning. It was an outdated setup, probably installed twenty or thirty years before the wars.

He ripped at vines choking a panel until he made out the imprint: *Sol-Tek Model III-B*. Probably South African, maybe third-generation beta. Even though the PV panels were damaged, there was still enough surface to generate juice.

He climbed down, brushed off his hands and smiled. "So far it looks good, Mr. Zingali."

"What tools you need to fix it?"

"Not much, yet. But first I have to see if the batteries are still sound." He tore vines from the shed entrance, then shouldered open the steel door and swiped at cobwebs.

Tomblike inside. Cool, with the stink of dust, mold, and mouse turds. Against the far wall the sine-wave inverter stood intact. It was an outdated 240-VAC system, but potentially could power a village twice this size. Next, the big test. He unlatched and pried up the lid of the battery housing. Spiders scurried and white powder billowed up.

Oh God. All six gel-matrix batteries were caked white, rotted through by corrosion. He shut the lid and leaned on the useless housing. How could he explain to Mr. Zingali and the others that this wasn't something he could fix? That no one could fix.

He took a breath, squared his shoulders and stepped outside.

Mr. Zingali cocked his head. "What be the matter? You can fix, yes?"

Jaym's voice caught. "I'm ... sorry, Mr. Zingali, but the batteries are ruined. They are the heart of the setup."

"But you know solar. You make them work".

Jaym lowered his voice. "Sir, the batteries are ... rotted. They're dead, forever. Nobody can fix them."

Mr. Zingali crossed his arms. "This is your duty for us. You find new batteries."

Jaym sensed the piercing eyes of the villagers. "I doubt there are any new batteries in the country."

Mr. Zingali shook his head and turned to the crowd. He waved an arm and shouted something in Chewan. Jaym watched Lingana and the others turn away and walk toward the village.

He stood alone. Hollow.

GIAMBO

"You are a laughingstock, people will always go laughing at you."

—East African proverb

After the villagers left Jaym in the field by the useless solar station, he could only stand there. He felt like an abandoned child wanting his mother.

Mom, he thought. She would have told him he did the best he could. She'd give him a hug and say, "Don't give up now! Show them what else you can do."

He never cried—not since Dad had left—but Jaym felt tears welling. He knew he shouldn't be such a baby, but here he was—alone, shunned, tens-of-thousands of kilometers from home. And he'd left Mom alone to sweat through endless days at work in her canary uniform. Jaym walked in circles in the morning heat for half an hour. Finally he worked up the courage to return to the village. He headed back slowly, but tried to keep his head high. Mom had always kept telling him not to slouch because it makes you look and feel like a loser. He might be one, but he had to try not to look like one in front of the village. He *did* do his best back there. No reason to—

Oh crap. Approaching the village he saw Mr. Zingali waiting on his porch. The old man jabbed his pipe stem at him. "What we gonna do with you, eh? You blenders s'posed to come and make things good for Africa. Fix things like they be before wars."

Jaym clenched his teeth. Would he always be shunned as the village idiot because he couldn't fix the unfixable? Couldn't they understand it wasn't his fault? "Sir, if the batteries weren't—"

Mr. Zingali waved him silent. "Since you cannot fix solar, for now you gonna work with son Giambo." The old man jabbed Jaym's bicep with his thumb. "You muscle be soft like girl. Giambo's work gonna make you strong."

Jaym rubbed his arm. "What's he gonna have me do?"

"He show you soon 'nough," said Mr. Zingali, shooing a pesky fly from his forehead.

As if on cue, a muscled African wearing only shorts limped toward them. He carried two pickaxes over his shoulder. He stopped an arm's length from Jaym, chin high, eyes narrowed. Jaym saw the same look of pride as Lingana's, but with a layer of bitterness—maybe hatred. He wanted to step back from Giambo but stood his ground. He'd keep eye contact, not show his fear.

"Giambo," said Mr. Zingali. "This be colony boy name Jay-em. We see if he better in you quarry than he do solar."

Jaym hesitated, then tentatively held out a hand. Giambo

looked aside and spat. Jaym lowered his hand and rubbed it on his shorts.

"Giambo not talk so much," said Mr. Zingali. He snapped at his son in Chewan. Giambo replied low and even, hissing the word, *mzungu*.

Mr. Zingali turned to Jaym, "Giambo say it be good that you work in quarry."

Right! thought Jaym. "I can use a pick. I'm...a little soft now, but in the Corridor I did a lot of—"

Giambo seized Jaym's wrist. He looked at Jaym's palm and shook his head. "Child hand. Fingers be ripe bananas. Think you be a tough *mzungu*?" He pushed one of the picks at Jaym's chest. "Yes, come. You dig and show us how you be strong NorthAm." He wheeled and limped down the hill.

Mr. Zingali shrugged. "He be a hard son. But he be good to mother and Lingana. Go with Giambo. Show him you dig much jade. Show him you be good 'nough for Lingana."

Lingana. At least he was still useful as her potential husband. Or was he just going to be a sperm donor as needed and shunned to live on the edge of the village? When Lingana had enough babies, then what? No, can't think like that. Gotta keep on task and earn their respect. Even acceptance.

He looked at his hands. "Sir? Do you have any...work gloves?"

Mr. Zingali chuckled. "Only city mzungu wear gloves. You go now, make skin tough like leather. Show village you be good at something." The old man hesitated. "It better if you be away from village most of day."

Why? wondered Jaym. *The shame of his solar failure?* He balanced the pickax on his shoulder and trod the kilometer down to the hillside quarry.

Giambo was already swinging his pick, back muscles rippling. He stopped and looked Jaym from head to toe and sneered. "Okay, colony boy. You dig there. Jade stones be in line of black rock." He pointed to a hand-width layer of shale running diagonally across the quarry wall. "Must chop 'way the gray rock to get at jade rock."

Jaym nodded, braced his legs, and swung the pick. The tip ricocheted in a shower of sparks. *Damn, it was like concrete.*

Giambo smirked. "'Ey, mzungu boy. Show off you muscle."

Jaym glared at the wall. He aimed, and swung, giving it all his back muscle. The pick bit in—a little. Five more grunting swings and a fist-sized chunk of overlay fell at his feet. Yes! He could do it.

"I be much impressed, colony boy. Ten more piece like that might be 'nough for few necklace beads."

Damn, thought Jaym. Is this the way it's going to be? Insulted every time he tried to do something with these people? Why couldn't they give him half a chance to prove himself? "How come you're so pissed off at me?" he snapped. "What have I done to you? Is it the solar thing? Because if it is, I—"

"Ooo. Blender boy angry?" Giambo took a step toward Jaym. He wanted to back away, but forced himself to stand his ground. Giambo's grin was menacing. "But maybe I be more angry." He leaned on his pick handle and stared through Jaym. "You ask what you done? It not be 'bout solar. It be that you blender peoples bring much, much trouble." His eyes burned into Jaym's. "Did not my father tell you 'bout my Nyanko?"

Jaym licked his cracked lips. "No."

"Is 'cause of you blender peoples I lose Nyanko. I never see her face again. Never hear her laugh." Giambo's face twisted; his eyes broke away from Jaym. "Nyanko my life. I gonna marry her." He looked across the quarry wavering with heat. "Was year ago. I visit Nyanko's parents in Sinaweh Village to talk 'bout bride price. But mzungu 'gades came. Sinaweh had a NorthAm blender, a boy like you. 'Gades find the blender and shoot him in village square."

Jaym took a breath. "Shot him?"

"Then they take girls with them. Three village girls and my Nyanko. Say it be lesson to other villages with blenders."

He watched Giambo's wild eyes. *Don't say anything now. Just let him talk.*

"I still see them," said Giambo. "White ghosts with devil eyes. Nyanko, she cry to 'gades. Tell them she gonna marry me. That we make no trouble." Giambo lowered his voice. "I beg to them like weak child. But they laugh. Use iron pipes to break legs. Now I walk crooked forever."

He glared at Jaym. "'Cause you come to Nswibe, there be danger for all in village."

"Yeah, there's risk, but without blenders, Africans are gonna die out."

"We die anyway. Blenders make mzungu babies."

Jaym shook his head. "Half African, half mzungu. African blood will survive with the children."

Giambo kicked at a rock. "'Nough talk." He walked to the quarry face. "Dig jade."

———————

At noon footsteps padded down the trail. Jaym squinted at the blurry figure. For the last hour his vision had wavered as he tried to blink away dark spots and flashes of light.

"Giambo. Jay-em," said Mr. Zingali. "Food ready in men's house."

Giambo brushed past Jaym and headed up the trail. Jaym steadied himself with the pick.

Mr. Zingali glanced at the pile of shale Jaym had chipped away. "Show me you hands."

Jaym moved a hand from the pick handle. Shreds of red skin peeled from his palm.

The older man grunted, then headed up the trail. Jaym dropped his pick and stumbled after him.

At the village Mr. Zingali pointed to a low adobe building. "Lingana cook in there. Tell her to medicine you hands." He turned and left.

Jaym steadied himself against the doorway. His dry voice rasped, "Lingana? You here?"

She stepped out, her face tight. "You should not be alone with me, Jay-em. Father will be angry if—"

"Your father told me to see you." He lifted his hands, palms out. "He asked you to patch me up."

Lingana looked at the oozing blood. Ribbons of skin dangled like red cloth.

"Come," she said. He followed her into the dim cooking shelter. "Sit."

Jaym plopped on the floor. A little girl watched from a shadow. "Is that one of your sisters?"

"Yes, youngest sister, Nabanda."

"Hi, Nabanda," smiled Jaym. The little girl made a shy grin and looked down. She'd have to be eleven or twelve, born just before the Flare.

"I never had a sister—or brother," he said.

"I think you must have family to be whole," said Lingana. "Or else you feel empty in your heart."

Jaym pursed his lips and made a quick shrug. Sure, he thought, it would be nice to have a family, but he'd been a Corridor rat and Mom was allowed only one child. And was he "empty in his heart"? He had no idea. Mainly he just felt kind of numb to most things.

Lingana took a small wood chest from a shelf. "Look like you butchered a goat. How did you tear your hands?"

"Using a pick in Giambo's quarry. My hands have gone soft." He tried to wipe sweaty hair from his eyes, but the touch flamed through his palm.

Lingana knelt and hesitantly took his hand.

Her slender fingers were cool on his. He couldn't remember the last time a girl had touched him. He was surprised at the tingle that rippled up his arm.

She shook her head. "Your flesh is too hot. You are not ready for this work, mzungu."

He tried to focus on her blurred face. "Back home...I worked this hard."

"This is not back home. How long do you work in sun?"

"Three, maybe four hours."

Lingana poured him a mug of grain beer. "Drink," she commanded. "Your lips bleed."

Bitter, but wet and cool. "Oh, man. Thank you."

Lingana frowned. "I am not a 'man.'"

"Sorry. That's just NorthAm slang." He wiped his chin with the back of a shaking hand.

From the medicine box Lingana unscrewed the lid of a small blue jar. She spoke in Chewan to her sister. Nabanda sprinted from the hut. Jaym leaned to look at the stuff in the jar. Thick as guacamole but with an eye-watering scent of sage and pepper.

Nabanda ran back inside with a damp rag in hand. Lingana dabbed at Jaym's palms. "Like skinned rabbit."

Jaym nodded, teeth gritted as she wiped at dried blood and caked dirt.

She frowned. "Why you do this, mzungu?"

Mzungu, he thought. Might as well say, *white guy who will always be an outsider.* "Um, could you please call me Jaym?"

She said nothing, but gently dabbed at his palm.

"It was your Dad's idea to work in the quarry. And I thought if I helped Giambo—"

"You cannot help Giambo."

"Cannot?"

She handed Nabanda the blood-and-dirt stained cloth and then dipped her fingers in the blue jar. She spread salve thick across his palm.

"Oh, geez!" gasped Jaym. He jerked his hand away. His eyes watered and his jaw trembled as the pain grew stronger. "Damn, damn, damn! That stuff is like acid!"

"It is good medicine," she said.

The pain eased to a numbing throb. He looked at his hands. Raw, but cleaned and greased with stuff that *had* to kill germs.

"That feels much better now. Thanks."

She turned away and fumbled the cap while resealing the jar. "You…must leave now. Go to men's house for meal."

She had hesitated, just for an instant. He tried to read her expression, but she busied herself with packing up the medicine kit. He nodded, stood, and slowly started outside. Jaym glanced back and saw her staring at him. When he caught her eye, Lingana's face seemed startled. She looked away.

He stepped into the afternoon heat and wandered toward the men's lodge for the evening meal. At the men's lodge they would make side-glances and mutter mzungu jokes. But he would go. He would show these villagers that he could take their crap—and more.

SHIELDS DOWN

Memo: SUN Office, Miz, to G.A. Hdqrs, Harare (6/8/69).

Highland raiders apparently have obtained electronic camouflage equipment from the black market. To eradicate their command base would take an estimated 75 Alliance Rangers. Presently there are only basic-trained GlobeTran troops in the region. The SUN mission in the Highlands must be tabled unless the Alliance Rangers can be secured.

Reya and the other camp women gathered outside the mess hall. The camp men inside still lay comatose from the scorpion root–spiked whiskey. There was no moon, only the haze of starlight for Reya to see the others. "Who brought the crowbar?" she asked.

A stocky woman handed her a meter-long bar. "Big 'nough?"

"Perfect, Kwentse. Okay, Zetta, get everyone in the Crawler and fire it up. Mai-Lin and I will come as soon as we finish with the com-shed."

Bare feet pattered toward the Crawler while Reya and

Mai-Lin sprinted to the communications shed. Reya jammed the bar's lip behind the lock and lunged. Wood splintered and bolts popped. The lock and hinge clattered to their feet.

Behind them they heard the churr-rrr-rr of the Crawler engine as Zetta struggled to start it. Reya held her breath and crossed herself. The engine finally caught and rumbled to life.

"Zetta did it!" said Mai-Lin.

"Thank God."

Inside the communications shed, they scanned the maze of computers, wiring, and blinking digital readouts on every table and shelf. "I have no clue which are the shield controls," said Reya. "We'll just take everything out." She swept the crowbar across the computer-lined tabletop. Glass and plastic shattered. Behind her, Mai-Lin snapped wires loose. They pitched computers, patchers, and coders to the floor. Machines sputtered and sparked.

Reya bashed the last flickering monitor. They crunched through debris and ran to the Crawler where the women pulled them aboard.

Reya slapped the cab and shouted above the engine roar. "Shields down. Drive, Zetta!" Gears ground. The Crawler lurched, but Zetta soon managed to smooth the machine to a steady pace. The women laughed and chirped victory yips and whistles.

The headlamps of the Crawler showed their way up the twisting muddy road and threw deep shadows into the forest ahead.

But they barely made it a kilometer. Then a blast.

When the explosion rocked the crawler, the women screamed. The vehicle bucked, then jerked to the right as the shattered left track uncoiled from its wheels. Zetta killed the engine and the women climbed out to see the damage. The track splayed on the muddy road like a metallic python. "Land mine," said Zetta.

"Dammit!" muttered Reya. She looked at the roadside. "There, that white boulder must mark the mine. Whole road might be mined. Okay, we've gotta—"

Zetta held up a hand. "Listen."

They froze. Reya sensed the subsonic hum—more like a vibration in her gut. "The Alliance drone is starting its pass," she whispered. Yes, she thought, and without the camp deflectors, the drone will finally see its target and unleash its rockets. "We're too close!" shouted Reya. "Everyone into the forest. Crouch behind a big tree. Cover your faces!"

The women scrambled through brush. Reya snapped through vines as the drone rumbled nearly overhead. She glanced over her shoulder to see four rockets flare from the drone's black silhouette.

The forest then lit as from a sudden sunrise.

"Down, down!" Reya screamed. She grabbed Mai-Lin's arm and yanked her behind a massive tree trunk. They clutched each other, kneeling low, eyes tight.

The explosion and blast wave ripped through the forest like a tornado. Reya's hair whipped her face. Limbs cracked and battered overhead. It sounded like bullets spattering into their tree.

The roar from the camp thundered across hills as debris began to fall. Shards of timber clattered through tree limbs. A fist-size piece of glowing metal thumped near Reya's foot. It sizzled in the damp moss.

Across the grove a woman screamed. Mai-Lin started to stand, but Reya jerked her back. "Not yet! Wait a few more seconds."

Clunk. The axle of a truck or crawler hissed just meters away. Then, quiet.

"Now," said Reya.

Mai-Lin and Reya ran toward the scream. One unbroken lantern glowed within the circle of women.

"Anyone hurt?" asked Reya.

"We are okay," said Zetta, "but look." She pointed to the ground. The stump of a scorched, smoldering arm lay in the grass. "Think it be Bossman arm?" asked Zetta.

"Could be anyone's," said Reya. She tried not to look at the severed end, the jagged bone.

"I think it be Bossman arm," said Zetta. "Poor, poor Bossman." She giggled. "Much pressure being boss. Make him fall to pieces." Women laughed nervously. Mai-Lin and Reya forced weak smiles.

"We gotta get out of here," said Reya. "If any outpost guards survived, they'll find the crawler and pick up our trail."

Zetta led the way with the lantern. "Step where I go," she said. "Easy to see mines on foot. There be one," she said, pointing to just a hint of mounded earth at the road's edge. A large white rock nearby confirmed it. The lantern swayed as they made their way in single file. They trudged on through the night, hearing animal cries and occasionally glimpsing pairs of glowing eyes.

Reya realized that the women would soon be parting, each heading for their own villages. She'd be alone. Mai-Lin might stick with her, or maybe she would go with Zetta, or another woman, to her village. But Reya had no destination except for the slim chance of finding D'Shay or Jaym. Jaym was her best chance. She'd never find D'Shay in his big city. Jaym's village was about seventy-five klicks west. Not impossible if she could skirt 'gades.

She wondered if those guys ever thought about her. They probably figured she was safe and happy with her blending match in a highland cabin. Maybe they had even tried to get in touch with her. If they did, the GlobeTran offices would say she went missing, then they'd figure she was dead.

But, what if *they* had been picked off by 'gades? If they were gone, what would she do? Could the 'gades be that much in control over here?

One thing for sure, she'd go down fighting before they took her prisoner again. No more being a slave and whore to a 'gade thug.

Within an hour the women reached a fork in the road.

"No road signs, so what now?" asked Reya.

"I know this place!" said Zetta excitedly. She pointed to the right-hand fork. "That way be west. My village be 'bout thirty klicks." She looked at Reya and the others.

"Come with me. My village called Mumbata. My people give you all shelter till you find new home."

The two tavern women stood apart. "What 'bout us?" asked one, her voice tight.

Zetta put her fists on her hips. "Can you get you hands dirty? Work like real woman?"

The two looked at each other, eyes wide. They nodded.

"Then come. We make real working women of you. No longer must rut with pigs."

"We should leave in twos," said Reya.

"Yes, good," said Zetta. "Better chance to hide from trouble if we not all together. Maybe Flora and I go first. Two more follow in five minutes. We now past land mines, so stay on road. It take you to my village, 'bout three, four hours. I be waiting."

The women hugged goodbyes and good-lucks before they paired off.

"Mai-Lin and I will be last," said Reya. "Go with God, Zetta, Flora. We'll see you at Mumbata."

Zetta and Flora trotted into the darkness.

Thirty minutes later, all the other women had gone. It was finally Reya and Mai-Lin's turn. They jogged and shuffled by starlight through the steamy night, brushing at mosquitoes and gnats. The road moved higher into an ancient forest with its open carpet of leaves and pine needles. Silhouettes of conifers and hardwoods loomed like silent statues.

Reya leaned against a tree. "Damn. I'm used up. Gotta rest for a few minutes."

"Good, 'cause I used too. Must take small rest."

They kicked together a bed of leaves and pine needles. Lying back to back, the girls fell asleep to the sounds of monkey cries, the buzz of mosquitoes, and the rhythm of crickets.

———————

Dawn crept through the forest canopy casting light and shadow across the forms of the two girls. A shaft of sunlight played across Reya's face. She started to cover her eyes with her arm, but sat bolt upright, her heart pounding. She shook Mai-Lin. "Wake up! We slept too long."

Mai-Lin blinked, then jumped up. Brushing off pine needles, she dashed to the edge of the glade—looking, listening like a small deer.

"You hear something?" asked Reya.

Mai-Lin's face was tight, pale. "Listen close. The only sound is small wind in treetops. But there are no birds singing. Too quiet. I think we must leave from here very fast."

REJECTION

To: SUN Headquarters, Geneva:
From: Global Alliance Headquarters, Harare.
[9 Aug. 2069]

We understand your concern that SUN
Peacekeepers in Africa are being recalled by
GlobeTran, Inc. However, our first goal in Africa
is to secure major African cities. Only then can we
expect to reclaim rural areas and resume the SUN
program.

A steaming hot Tuesday morning marked Jaym's second week of work in Giambo's quarry. Blood no
longer spotted his bandaged palms and he was building
calluses—and some shoulder muscle.

He and Giambo worked in the blistering sun until
noon, then without a glance at Jaym, Giambo laid his pick
aside and headed up the trail for the midday meal. Jaym
dropped his pick and inspected his pile of ore. Only about
half of Giambo's, but not bad. Yesterday Giambo looked
at Jaym's day's work and made a brief nod. Jaym had felt a
surprising flush of pride.

Heading into the village he saw kids playing with each other, women working with women, men chatting with men. It had taken some gut-clenching courage, but a few times he tried to ease into a group of guys and greet them a respectful *Lowane*. In their eyes he might be a solar failure, but maybe he could get them to warm up to him a bit, to show them he was trying to pick up a few words of Chewan, and hope they'd quit looking at him like a leper. But so far it was no good. The guys would stop talking when he approached them. After a few sly glances toward him, one would mutter something in Chewan. The others would smirk at Jaym.

Probably telling mzungu light-bulb jokes, like; *How many mzungus does it take to screw in a light bulb? Why bother? No solar, so no electricity! Ha ha.* Maybe in time they'd get tired of it. Maybe in time he could learn Chewan. Right. And maybe in time he'd sprout wings and fly back to NorthAm.

NorthAm. He never thought he'd miss the dusty, sweaty Corridor, but he was so alone here. Back home he'd at least be able to talk with Mom, even a passing neighbor.

Mom. She'd probably be sleeping now. Up in a few hours to dress in that yellow uniform. Even as pathetic as his Corridor life had been, it had been a comforting familiarity. Not like here where he had to weigh every word he spoke.

Jaym stood back from half a dozen village kids playing a Chewan version of hopscotch with squares scratched in the dust. He'd like to show them his Corridor version, but if he talked with the kids, he knew the guys would really have something to yuck about. Maybe even think he was a pervert.

"Jay-em," whispered Lingana. She stood behind him, shadowed in a doorway, a basket of corn balanced against her slim hip.

She looked like a slender dancer in silhouette. For a moment he forgot that she was an African girl. At that moment she was a graceful young woman looking at him with that open gaze of hers.

He tried to sound breezy. "Hey, Lingana."

She hesitated, eyes down now. "I am not to talk to you alone, but you must hear a very ... serious thing."

Jaym tensed. "Okay."

"I think you must go from Nswibe ... forever."

It was like a punch in his gut. He had to wait a couple of breaths before he could reply. "But ... why?"

She spoke softly yet firmly. "You must go. Because ..." She looked to one side. "Because you do not belong here."

He felt dropped through a trapdoor. Any hope he had nursed of fitting in over here evaporated. He pulled off his cap and pushed back sweat-tangled hair. His voice wavered. "Geez, Lingana, I've tried my best. Even Giambo is starting to—"

"No. I think you do not understand. It is too dangerous. Dangerous for my village." Her face softened. "And for you."

"The 'gades?"

She nodded. "You know Giambo's story. Long as you are here, no one is safe. 'Specially you."

"But the Alliance soldiers will protect your village. They've sent thousands of the military over here."

She shook her head. "We see no soldiers."

Jaym pulled his hat back on. "I could go to the city and tell the Alliance people what's happening. They'd get soldiers out—"

"Alliance people all replaced by GlobeTran now. Their office people just make you fill out forms. Say they send soldiers, but no one comes. I think they care nothing for us."

"Do the SUN people know about this?"

"We used to see SUN people visit villages, but they have not come for many weeks." She pointed her chin to the west, toward the haze of mountains. "We hear there is one place where you find safety. That is where you must go. It is a place for blenders and people who believe in SUN. They are a mix, white and brown. You go there and my village will be safe." She paused and glanced to one side. "Also you."

"But I don't want to spend my life hiding in hills." He wanted to add, *maybe I could become a part of this place. And maybe you could see me as myself—not as an interfering mzungu.*

"Jay-em, those in the hills do not hide. They are a growing colony called *New SUN*." Lingana's face was eager now. Her voice filled with a new passion. "Yes, New SUN wants the blending to succeed and fight the 'gades. They will sweep them from Africa."

Footsteps, just behind them.

"Father comes." Lingana whirled away.

Jaym reached out to touch her arm, but she was gone.

D'SHAY'S DECISION

"If men swear that they want to harm you when you are asleep, you can go to sleep. If women say so, stay awake"

—*African proverb*

———————

After Pop and Gemmit left the tavern, D'Shay and Charles played a couple of games of pool on the warped table beneath a bare light bulb.

"Closing time," hollered the bartender. She shook a man slumped at the bar. "Wake, wake, Josef."

"You need help, Mala?" asked Charles.

"Thank you, no. You and brown mzungu friend gather pool balls and go home too."

Home, thought D'Shay as he fetched an errant ball from under a table. Home meant Philira. How could SUN screw up so badly? His "Blending Program" pamphlet had said over 50 traits were matched with each Blending couple. It explained that "thorough research has demonstrated 90 percent of blending pairs would be satisfied with their matches." Either a pile of bull, or he was one of the 10 percent to be matched with an ogre.

The bartender, solid as Philira, but with wide, sexy eyes, hoisted the drunk by his shirt and dragged him to the door. She gave him a good shoulder shake. "You able to walk now, Josef? You wife gonna skin you if you don't get home. Now shoo!"

Josef made a leering grin before he swayed out the door. "You boys!" Mala shouted. "Out, out! You stay longer and I make you clean toilet room."

Back at the house Charles unlocked the front door and they crept in. D'Shay heard Philira's rhino snorts three rooms away.

Lantern light shone from the kitchen. "Is Pop waiting up?" asked D'Shay.

"No. He always hit bed fast when home." Charles stepped through the kitchen door. "Chirilie? What you doing up so late?"

She was in an oversized yellow robe, sipping tea. She looked at Charles and D'Shay. "I wait to tell DuShay 'bout … big problem."

D'Shay shuddered. "Is it Philira?"

She nodded. "I hear her talk to street boy on porch tonight. She give him money."

Charles rubbed his chin. "What you hear?"

Chirilie looked at her teacup. D'Shay saw a tear glisten in her eye. "The boy said they gonna do it Friday, on you way home from work."

D'Shay, stunned, plopped down next to Chirilie. *Damn,* he thought. Sure, Gorilla-Girl was nasty—but to put a contract on him? And the killer, or killers, could be anyone in the bustle of the streets. Maybe somebody looking like a street vendor, or even a beggar. Be so easy for someone in a crowd to pass by and push a shiv between his ribs, then just keep walking. He shuddered at the thought of bleeding to death on a cobbled African street while curious passersby paused to watch.

"Two days," sighed Charles. "We only got two days to make plan for you, DuShay."

D'Shay squeezed Chirilie's hand. "They won't get me, Sweet Girl. Back home I've dealt with worse than these alley rats." But back home he knew the faces of his enemies. It was an all-new game over here.

"What you gonna do, DuShay?" asked Chirilie. "They maybe come in two, three, maybe four. Cannot fight all."

Charles nodded. "She be right. You might win one alley boy, but they work in pack like hyenas."

"You must leave," whispered Chirilie.

"Run?" said Charles. "You think DuShay run like rabbit? *No!* DuShay be a man. He must not run. We figure out how he win and save honor."

"Can I have a sip of your tea, Sweet Girl?" asked D'Shay.

She pushed her cup across the table. He drank half the bitter liquid and grinned.

"What you smiling 'bout?" asked Charles. "You must be serious, DuShay. We plan a fight 'gainst alley boys. Gemmit, you, me. We wait and make ambush Friday."

D'Shay shook his head. "Sorry, Chaz. But I'm really not into the honor thing. Did you know my middle name is Rabbit?"

Chirilie and Charles stared at D'Shay. "You make joke?" asked Charles.

"Yeah, it's a joke. But not much. I'm not gonna fight those punks. One of you guys could get really hurt, and even if we won, Philira will try something else. Look, I want to keep these rabbit ears of mine. I'll have to try my luck someplace else. Maybe I can find a girl who won't sic alley rats after me."

Charles crossed his arms, his nostrils flared.

"Don't look at me like that, Chaz. Honor is good and all, but me taking off won't dishonor your family. I'm gonna save my honor for another time—not waste it on street boys."

Charles pushed his chair back. "I go to bed." He shook his finger. "You think hard on this, DuShay. Dishonor follow you like bad spirit." He stormed from the kitchen.

D'Shay looked at Chirilie. "How do you feel about this honor stuff, Pretty Girl? You think I'm a chicken?"

She smiled. "You not chicken, you be rabbit. And honor be for boys who forget what be important in life."

"Girl, you're smarter than the whole bunch put together."

She blushed, then looked up. "I gonna help you be best rabbit in city."

———

Thursday night. The family was sleeping when D'Shay met Chirilie back in the kitchen. The lantern was turned low and Chirilie was flattening a wrinkled sheet of paper.

"Hey, Sweet Girl."

"Hey, DuShay," she grinned.

"What's the paper and pencil for?"

"I gonna draw map for rabbit trail. You say you have blender friend in close by village?"

"Yeah. It's called Nswibe. He said it was north of here."

"Yes, tiny village in pretty valley. I have Auntie in Zobua Village near Nswibe."

"Is there a way I can contact Nswibe and talk to my friend?"

"There be a communication center near Father's shop, but many village coms broken. We cannot make contact Auntie in Zobua. I see her last year and she say 'gade people cut com wires. Zobua and Nswibe probably be on same com line. I think you must walk and trust God."

"Okay, I just hope God is watching this rabbit."

"God watch all rabbits. Here, I draw you the way." She sketched a rectangle at the bottom of the paper. "This be our city, Wananelu." She made a tiny "x" in the upper left corner of the rectangle. "Our house be 'bout here. Now watch how you get to Nswibe Village."

After half an hour of penciling the streets and lettering in their names, Chirilie grinned and held the map to D'Shay. "Is the map good?"

"Better than any treasure map. Best map I've ever

seen." He hugged Chirilie and pecked a kiss on her cheek. "I'm gonna miss you, Sweet Girl."

"Miss you too, DuShay Rabbit. What you gonna do at new village? Help peoples make things better? That what blenders do, yes?"

D'Shay shrugged. "We'll see. I gotta help myself first. Need to look out for Number One. Me."

She blinked. "It be good to look out for others too. So also help person Number Two and Three, yes?"

D'Shay nodded. "You're a wise girl, Chirilie. I'll remember your words."

She gave him a weak smile. "Good. And maybe write to me letter when you be safe? And you tell me all the good things you do for village peoples."

"Sure, you bet. And for you I'll put flowers and hearts on the envelope."

She giggled.

———

Before dawn D'Shay crept into the dark living room and listened. All was quiet, except for MonstaGirl's snorks. From Chirilie and Grammy's room drifted Grammy's occasional whimpers and toothless babble

He'd miss Chirilie and the guys. Especially sweet little Chirilie. Good name. She was always cheery, no matter if Philira was having a tantrum, or if Grammy messed her drawers during breakfast. If only he could get her out of here and give her a jump-start to a better life

He went back to the kitchen and labored to write a goodbye note to the little girl. The note had lots of pencil erasing before he finished, but it had to do. He read it once more before he folded the paper:

Sweet Chirilie,

I hate to leave because I'm really going to miss your smile and your fine cooking.

Here are two pieces of D'Shay wisdom:

(1) Don't let Big Sister boss you around.

(2) Have Pop and the boys get you into school. Chaz and I have talked about it, and we agree you have the family brains and a chance to make it clear to college. Chaz promised he will work on Pop.

Chirilie, you are a smart, wonderful girl. Stay strong.

Your Mzungu Brother, D'Shay Rabbit

He glanced out the kitchen window. 0430 and already the sky was showing a pink tinge of twilight. A rooster crowed as D'Shay quietly filled his water bottle. He poked through the cupboard and found some honey-sweetened corn bars—a Chirilie specialty.

He laid his pack by the back door then looked into the room where Chirilie and Grammy slept. The little girl's mouth was open in sleep, one arm tucked under her cheek. Carefully, carefully he slid his folded note under a corner of her pillow.

Back in the kitchen, he hefted his pack and held the handle of the screen door. He waited. As the rooster gave a full-throttled wake up call, he yanked open the squeaky door and slipped out. Nobody in sight. Just birds squawking and dogs yapping. He slipped around the house and headed up the empty side street. There he checked Chirilie's map.

It took him an hour to get to the outskirts of Wananelu. He spotted a faded road sign: *Prince Nebia Ave.* Good, that was on her map. He was heading the right direction.

By now people were up starting their chores and making trips into town. He passed women in bright wraparounds carrying impossible loads—water jugs, bundles of firewood, baskets of yams. A lot of women in this country were damn good-looking—fine cheekbones, big eyes, slender bodies. He flashed his smile and nodded at the younger ones. "*Lowane*, miss. How ya doing, sugar." They passed without giving him a look. *Give it up*, he thought. *Save your charm for a Nswibe girl.*

On the far edge of the city he reached the bullet-pocked church marked on the map—a brick building with a rusty tin roof and a crooked little steeple. A forest of small, white crosses sprouted beside the church. A cemetery of Eleven-Effect babies? At the church the road branched. D'Shay glanced at the map. Chirilie had penciled the right-hand fork with an arrow and the words, *Nswibe, about 10 k?*

Okay, time to stretch out the legs.

In the baking heat of late afternoon, D'Shay leaned against a roadside tree to rest his wobbling legs. No leaves, but the fat trunk threw shade across his sizzling hide. The deserted road appeared to ribbon endlessly into low hills. Only cicadas buzzed in the grass while a formation of vultures circled high above the stubbled plain. He mopped sweat from his face. He'd come at least ten, maybe fifteen klicks and should be to Nswibe by now. And why no people on the road? Was this a no-man's area? Maybe 'gade territory?

He stiffened at the sound of an approaching car. He turned to see a racing plume of dust coming his way. Yes! A chance to hitch a ride to Nswibe. Except, who would be out here driving like a maniac? Cops? 'Gades? Better wait behind the tree to get a good look at the rig before sticking out his thumb. 'Gades would likely be in pairs, maybe in a Rover, or a pickup with a mounted machine gun. He crouched as the rig neared.

It was a white Rover, coming fast. Only one driver. The white paint usually meant a government car, maybe a GlobeTran rig. Still could be dangerous, but he had to take the chance. He was out of water, and the road was endless. He ran to the roadside and waved his arms.

The Rover's brakes squealed. As the dust cloud drifted past, D'Shay saw the uniformed driver. A girl! "Damn!" he whispered.

The uniformed girl frowned. "Why do you curse?"

Okay, time to turn on the charm. "Sorry, miss... ma'am.

I'm just a little overwhelmed. Most of the police I've seen haven't been so—gorgeous—if you'll forgive me saying so."

A slight smile, just for an instant. His flattery was working. But it wasn't hard to lay it on thick because she really was fine looking. Flawless chocolate skin and lips to make any guy weak-kneed.

"I am not police. I am a SUN liaison officer, but I have police authority. What are you doing out here? This is empty land."

"I'm trying to find my assignment village. Nswibe."

"Do you know this area is infested with 'gades?"

"I've heard they're around . . . so maybe you could give me a lift to Nswibe?"

She held out her hand. "Show me your assignment card."

"Oh, yeah—sure. You're the first real SUN person I've seen since I've been over here. Mostly I've run into G-T contractors. I'm a SUN blender, so you and I are—"

"Or maybe you be a deserter looking to join some 'gades?" She snapped her fingers. "Your card!"

Have to stall. If she knew I'm running from my Wananelu assignment, I might be in it deep. "Hey, no. I hate 'gades." He dug through his pockets, frowning. "Hope I didn't lose my tags. Sometimes I—"

"Now!"

He tried to act calm as he handed over his holo card. She lifted her sunglasses and tapped the card.

She narrowed her eyes and waved his holo card like a fan. "I am disappointed that you tell me lies, Mr. D'Shay

Green from NorthAm. It shows here you are assigned to Wananelu City."

He feigned a defeated smile. "Yeah, I didn't quite tell you all the truth. Look—I had big trouble in Wananelu. My blending match was, um—unhappy with me. Unhappy enough to hire a street gang to cut me up."

"Why did you not report this to authorities in Wananelu?"

"What authorities? The SUN and Alliance Offices in Wananelu have GlobeTran signs on the doors. And if SUN is really still trying to do the blending thing, I don't think their headquarters—wherever it is—knows what's really happening over here."

She pursed her lips. "Yes, the SUN presence has been sourced out to GlobeTran. There are many decent soldiers in GlobeTran uniforms, but officials hold them back. They should be out here eliminating the 'gades. But GlobeTran wants them policing the cities. I am one of the few remaining SUN agents working in the field. One by one we are being recalled to the cities to work under GlobeTran supervisors." She sighed. "But it does little good to complain about things one cannot change."

D'Shay shaded his eyes, sweat dripping from his face. "Do you mind if I sit in the car? I'm broiling in this sun."

She cocked her head, reading his face. "Yes, but do not make trouble. I am armed and an expert with a pistol."

He held his palms up. "I just want shade, and I'd sure appreciate a ride to Nswibe. Please." He gingerly opened the door and slid into the passenger seat. Her left hand gripped a stubby pistol. He cleared his throat and smiled. "Just trust me. I'm a good guy. No need for the gun."

"Place your pack in the back seat." Still unsmiling, she holstered the pistol and shifted into low. "I am also a karate black belt, so keep your hands in your lap and be the good blender boy you say you be."

"Yes, ma'am. Whatever you say."

"Why do you want to go to Nswibe? It be a tiny village."

"I have a blender friend who's assigned there. I thought his village might take me in until I figure out what to do next."

"What to do next? Should be no doubt! You come here for SUN blending mission, yes? And you bring training to help Africa. Also be here to make babies for African girl, correct?"

"Uh, sure. I'm here to do all that."

She smirked.

"Hey, you gotta believe me. You think I'm only out for myself?"

"That is for you to decide." She slid on her sunglasses and did a U-turn in the road. She pointed with her chin. "Nswibe in those hills, maybe five kilometers."

"I'm sure grateful for the ride … Miss—or is it Mrs.?"

"I am not married. A SUN officer cannot marry while in service." She waited a few moments before saying, "You may call me Nakhoza."

ZIG AND ZAG

To: Global Alliance Headquarters, Harare
From: GlobeTran, Ltd, Chewena Office
Re: Rural renegade activity

Despite unfounded complaints from a few former
SUN field officers, GlobeTran personnel have
neutralized renegade activities in rural areas of
the country. The SUN Blender Program is in no
danger.

Reya heard men's voices down the trail. She crouched
with Mai-Lin behind a fern-shrouded stump. Reya
glanced back, looking for better cover. Dense brush lay
at the forest's edge, maybe fifty meters upslope, but only
patches of grass sprouted between here and the tree line.

Through the ferns, Reya watched two men in camos,
armed and moving their direction. One stopped and kneeled,
scanning the path like a scout.

"You think they camp men?" whispered Mai-Lin.

"Yeah, probably guards on remote outpost."

"We must run," said Mai-Lin. She looked up the hill.
"If we reach brush, the forest hide us."

"Too far in the open. They'll shoot us down if we run. Listen—I'm gonna talk to them. Whoever they are, I can BS our way past them."

Mai-Lin shook her head. "No!" she whispered. "That suicide."

"I can get through this." Reya fingered the knife on her hip. "They won't know me. We've got no choice, so stay low and don't move till I signal to come out."

Mai-Lin clutched at her arm.

"I'll be okay." Reya pulled away and stepped into the clearing. Hands raised, she walked slowly toward the two men, hoping they didn't see her fear, her quaking hands.

They raised their rifles and shouted in Chewan.

"Take it easy, men!" She forced back a surge of panic. She smiled and veed her fingers in peace. "I just...wanna talk."

"Keep you hands in air, bitch girl." They moved warily toward her.

"I don't know what's going on, but I—"

"Shut up, mzungu filth. You one of bitches who blow up camp."

She shook her head, took a step back and felt for her knife.

"Hand off knife, girl, or I shoot you legs. Not ready to kill you, yet." He told the other man, "Tape her mouth and wrists behind back. Not ankles." He grinned. "You know why we leave you ankles free?"

Reya spun and sprinted. "Mai-Lin, run!"

Mai-Lin leaped up and bolted uphill.

A bullet hissed past Reya's ear followed by the crackle of more gunfire.

"Zigzag!" panted Reya. "Duck and dodge! You hear?"

Mai-Lin's short legs pumped. She stayed ahead of Reya. "Zig and zag!"

Bursts of shots. Bullets buzzed like bees, spattered dirt.

A bullet tugged at Reya's shirtsleeve. She glanced over to see Mai-Lin sprinting and dodging like a champ. Brush and forest lay a few meters away.

Mai-Lin's arms flew up like a bird taking flight.

"Mai-Lin!" screamed Reya. She caught the falling girl in her arms and kept running. Sweat stung her eyes, blurred the brush ahead.

A swat in her arm, a white flare of pain.

Mai-Lin flopped against her like a limp doll. Reya hit the brush sideways, shouldering through the mat of brambles and vines. A spray of bullets snapped twigs and branches. She pushed and twisted deep into the thicket. Behind her the shouts of the men now sounded more distant. The bursts of gunfire sporadic. She pushed on, thorns clawing at her face, tearing at the flesh of her arms and legs. The men would not follow them through this vicious tangle. They know we are wounded and will bleed to death in the forest.

"We've escaped," she said to Mai-Lin. Her hand pressed Mai-Lin's face to Reya's breastbone. The thorns would not scratch her friend's face.

———

After nightfall Reya continued to stagger past trees and through brush in tree-slatted moonlight. Her gun-shot arm dangled, throbbing with hot pain. Her arms and legs trickled with blood and burned from the fire of the thorns. Her good arm ached and trembled under the weight of Mai-Lin's limp form.

The trill of crickets and calls of forest animals were muffled by her own heartbeats drumming in her ears. But, there! Not far ahead—the flicker of cooking fires. Thank God. A tiny village in the middle of the forest. "Mai-Lin," she rasped. "We're almost there."

Nearing a cabin of corrugated tin she cried weakly, "Help us. Please ... help." Her knees buckled. She knelt in the dirt. "Please ..."

When Reya collapsed, she still clutched Mai-Lin to her breast.

UNEXPECTED
VISITORS

When arriving at your Blending assignment,
be sure not to startle villagers by bursting in
unannounced. Unannounced visitors in rural areas
may be seen as a potential threat that could put a
Blender in harm's way and may jeopardize his or
her mission.

—*Blender Handbook, chapter 14, "Village Customs"*

Jaym had lost count of the days since his arrival in
Nswibe. Why count? It was easier just to try to flow
with the routine of life and work here. Get out of bed at
dawn, eat a bowl of corn gruel and have some tea, then go
off to work in the quarry.

On this morning he walked through patches of ground
fog. At first glance the fog reminded him of the Corridor
inversion layers, when all the dust and smoke from brush
fires settled low and toxic across the sprawl. But here you
could breath in lungfuls of this crisp, white fog. A sudden breeze hushed down the canyon and the mists swirled
away to expose the cobalt African sky.

These moments of calm and peace helped ease the pain of Lingana's ultimatum. Okay, he'd have to leave eventually, but until then he'd focus on this daily routine that had become kind of a comfort. Whatever happened, he would take with him these moments of having a purpose and gradually being accepted by the villagers.

Jaym looked at his leathered palms and rubbed the soreness in his arms. He ached every day, but it wasn't as bad as that killer first week. This was the end of week three; swinging a pick had built muscle, and he didn't quake like jelly at day's end. He could do this, and he had learned that swinging the pick with all his might wasn't the trick. After lots of trial and error, he found that there was some Zen to this business. The trick was hitting at the right angle—at exactly that sweet spot between the ore and overlay.

At the quarry the fog had swirled upslope, forming fleeting clouds against the cliff. There was Giambo, early as usual, already hacking out ore. Giambo glanced up and nodded. "*Lowane*," he murmured low.

Giambo said hello! Had he earned a little respect because he could now pile up a decent heap of ore at day's end? "Lowane, Giambo." But Giambo had already turned back to his work, pick swinging in his endless rhythm. Oh well. There was little he could really talk about with Giambo anyway. Besides, he needed a morning of work and sweat to dull the anxiety of leaving.

Jaym and Giambo had dug for an hour when they turned to the sound of footsteps pattering down the trail.

It was Lingana's little sister, Nabanda. She burst out a rapid string of Chewan words, then she and Giambo stared at Jaym. "Strangers come," said Giambo.

Jaym's gut tightened. "'Gades?"

Giambo said nothing, but his face hardened. He took a fighter's stance, bracing his feet and gripping his pick, ready to swing.

Footsteps pounded down the trail. *Oh God*, thought Jaym. He glanced at the grove of trees down the trail. If he sprinted, he might—

"Do not run like a sheep," said Giambo. "Stand with me like a man. Nabanda," he commanded the little girl. "Hide behind those rocks and make no sound. Do not come out until someone from village comes for you." Nabanda hesitated, then sprinted to hide behind a pile of boulders at the quarry's edge.

Jaym shuddered as he gripped his pick tighter. In those last seconds he thought of his mom. She'd never know how or where he died. And what about Lingana? What would they do to her? He moved closer to Giambo and took his stance. Maybe the two of them could take out a couple of 'gades before—

"Jaymster!" shouted D'Shay as he rounded the trail and jogged into the quarry.

Jaym's jaw dropped. He tossed down his pick. "Damn! You could have shouted a warning. We thought you were 'gades."

Giambo glared at the two. "Hey, Giambo," said Jaym.

"This is my friend, D'Shay, a blender friend stationed in Wananelu."

Giambo cocked his head. "Brown blender? There be brown peoples in NorthAm?"

D'Shay walked over to Giambo and held out his hand. "D'Shay Green here."

Giambo looked at the hand, and finally gave D'Shay a light handshake.

"Yeah," said D'Shay. "There's lots of us brown folks in NorthAm."

Nabanda slowly moved from the rocks into the open.

"And who is this beautiful girl?" asked D'Shay.

"Nabanda," she said softly, shyly sliding behind Giambo.

Giambo glared. "She not be old 'nough for you."

"Hey, no. I'm just being friendly. She reminds me of a little girl in my Wananelu family."

Giambo's face softened a little. "If you be brown blender, then you make brown babies with African woman, yes?"

D'Shay glanced to Jaym. "Is that a big deal here, Jaymo? They been giving you a bad time for being white?"

Jaym shrugged. "It's complicated. Tell you later."

D'Shay put his fists on his hips and looked Jaym up and down. "Look at you. You've got a real tan, and is that actual muscle I see on your arms? Lordy, you're a new man, Jaymster."

Jaym struck a muscleman pose with jutted jaw and flexed biceps. D'Shay laughed and Nabanda giggled. Even Giambo made a half grin.

"How did you get here, D'Shay? You take a couple of vacation days?"

"Uh, not exactly. I'm sort of AWOL at the moment. A pretty lady picked me up on the road, and here I am. She's in the village getting a bite to eat. You gotta meet her."

"I wish I had your way with women."

"You got your own lady here, right?"

Jaym saw Giambo watching them. "That's also complicated."

"Is Giambo your boss?" whispered D'Shay.

"Yeah."

"Say, Giambo," said D'Shay. "Is it okay for Jaym here to take a little break?"

Giambo shrugged. "Take 30 minute, but you must work half hour late tonight."

Jaym leaned his pick against the quarry wall. "Thanks, Giambo. Back in thirty." Jaym pulled on his dusty tee shirt and headed up the trail with D'Shay.

"Man," said D'Shay, "bet he's a lot of fun to work for."

"He's okay. Been through a lot. 'Gades took his fiancée. He's got reason to be angry. Thought he was gonna cut my throat at first, but we're getting along better."

"That's why I skipped out of Wananelu," said D'Shay. "My bride-to-be was not pleased to be matched with my skin tone, as gorgeous as it is. She wanted a lily-white boy. She put a price on my head, so I'm on the run from street thugs."

At the village, Jaym saw Lingana talking with a girl

in a SUN uniform. He nodded toward them. "That's my blending match. Lingana."

"Very nice, Jaymster. A petite beauty."

"Truth is, she wants me gone."

"'Cause you're white?"

"No. She worries that I'm gonna bring 'gades down on the village. I guess they're thick in this part of the country. When they come, they do more than just take down the blender." He rubbed his scalp. "She wants me to go to the mountains and join some colony."

"Have other villagers told you to leave?"

"Not really. Giambo's talked about 'gade danger. He knows I'm 'gade bait."

"Hey," said D'Shay, "I wouldn't leave this place unless they threw me out bodily. Your blending match is too good-looking and the village looks pretty sweet."

Jaym nodded. "I'm starting to feel more a part of this place. And, yeah, she is good-looking. And smart. But..."

"Yes, you are smitten. You're not going anywhere buddy. 'Specially now that I'm here. We little lost blenders gotta stick together."

Jaym grinned. He nodded toward the girl talking with Lingana. "Who's the gal in the uniform? A SUN cop?"

"That's my Madonna-of-the-Dusty-Road. Name's Nakhoza. She's a genuine SUN officer and saved me from the vultures and 'gades. She's one of the few SUN people that haven't been replaced by a GlobeTran scab."

"Does she know you're on the run from Wananelu?"

"Yeah. Nakhoza knows that a lot of blenders don't fit

the slots the Alliance assigned us. Plus she's ticked off that the Alliance outsourced their missions to GlobeTran. And it seems G-T has pretty much abandoned any SUN goals, at least in the Chewena countryside. But, hey—let's have some introductions before your break is over."

They walked over to the girls. Jaym noticed that Nakhoza was half a head taller than Lingana.

"Nakhoza," said D'Shay, "this is my buddy, Jaym." They made awkward smiles and shook hands.

"And Lingana, this is D'Shay. We sailed here in the same ship."

Lingana bowed her head slightly and shook his hand. "Pleased to meet you."

The four stood silent for a moment. Finally Nakhoza said, "Lingana asks me to stay for evening meal. That is very kind." She toed the dirt. "I do not have much chance to be social with people. I hope my uniform does not disturb others."

"I have told our people that you are with SUN," said Lingana. "They know SUN tries for doing good in Africa."

Jaym noticed Lingana avoiding eye contact with him. He cleared his throat. "I gotta get back to work. Nice to meet you Nic.. "

"Nakhoza," smiled the SUN girl. "It must be a hard name for NorthAms."

"It's a nice name," said Jaym. "I just, um ... I gotta get back to the quarry. I'll see you all at mealtime."

"Or half an hour later," reminded D'Shay.

"Right, right." Jaym turned and headed down the trail.

ELEPHANT

Elephant: A now-extinct ungulate mammal of
great size. The last known elephant was killed in
2053 during the Pan-Af Wars. Elephants are still a
fetish creature for several African tribes who revere
the animal's renowned strength and intelligence.

—*GlobaPedia, vol. 3, p. 132*

Reya fluttered her eyes open to focus on a ceiling of
thatched reeds. Her head throbbed. Her mouth was
cotton dry. She blinked, trying to focus, to remember. Her
hands fingered a woven mat beneath her. Overhead a small
lizard scampered upside down. She half smiled. A pretty
little creature dappled in yellow and white. It searched for
insects, jerking like a 'lectro toy. A gecko of some kind.
Yeah. Her little sister once had a pet gecko back in—

Images and sounds tumbled back. Running, panting.
Shooting.

Her voice rasped, "Mai-Lin?" When she elbowed herself up, a bolt of pain flamed through her arm. Reya gasped,
waiting for waves of red to subside. She looked around the
hut lit only by a gas lantern. "Mai-Lin!"

A withered black woman with cropped salt-and-pepper hair stepped into the room. *"Muli bwanji?"*

"I—don't understand. Do you speak English? World-Speak?"

The woman shrugged. *"Sindikunva. Dzina lako ndani?"*

Reya pointed to herself, then out the door. "Mai-Lin? Other girl? Where is the other girl?"

The woman squatted beside her. *"Sindikunva."* She lifted Reya's bandaged arm.

"Anngh! Oh, God that hurts."

The old woman nodded, then unwound part of the bandage. Reya looked down at her upper arm and nearly blacked out. Her flesh looked like chunks of meat sewn together with fishing line. A zombie arm. The bullet looked like it had ripped through her bicep with enough force to also mangle and displace her tricep. She knew if it had hit bone she'd have no arm.

The old woman hummed as she dabbed at the puckered, oozing wounds with a damp cloth. She smiled at Reya and proudly pointed to the stitching. *"Chabwino. Chabwino."*

Reya grimaced. "Yes, yes, *chabwino.*"

The woman unscrewed the lid from an old mustard jar. The stuff inside was a muddy purple. She globbed it on her fingers and rubbed it onto Reya's stitches.

"Aiiie! Oh *geez!* Please, lady!"

"Chabwino," whispered the woman. She rewound the bandage and pinned it in place.

Reya gritted her teeth and tried to sit up further. The pain was electric and made her eyes water.

The woman motioned to the mat. *"Iyayi, iyayi!"*

"No, I gotta get up," said Reya, rolling on her side. She reached out to the woman. "Please. I have to see Mai-Lin."

"Iyayi! Ukupita kuti?"

Reya struggled to her knees. The woman took Reya's hand and steadied her to her feet.

A small girl with black hair entered the room.

"Mai-Lin?"

The girl stepped into the lantern light.

Not Mai-Lin. Reya's knees buckled, but the old woman steadied her.

"¿Hablas español?" asked the girl.

"Sí," Reya said softly. They continued in Spanish. "Mai-Lin's ... dead, isn't she?"

"Please, lie back on the mat."

Reya grimaced as the old woman helped her down to the mat.

"Ndatopa," muttered the woman as she limped from the room.

"Gonani bwino, Amai," replied the girl. She knelt by Reya. "I am Bettina. Like you, I am a blender. My home was Bolivia."

The language of Reya's grandmother flowed easier now. Somehow it seemed right for this pain and loss. *"Me llamo Reya. Soy de MexiCal."* The soft syllables brought a swirl of memories of girlhood. Of her small grandmother— her *abuelita*—slapping out tortillas and humming in the kitchen. The smells of cinnamon and vanilla. Of pork frying with chilies. The sound of the old clock ticking and bonging in the dining room.

Reya took Bettina's wrist, searched her eyes. "Please, tell me about Mai-Lin."

Bettina rubbed the back of Reya's hand. "The bullet tore her heart. No pain or suffering. Your friend is with God." She crossed herself.

Reya wiped tears. "It's my fault. We escaped from a 'gade camp, but they caught us. I thought I could talk our way past them." She shivered at the memory of Mai-Lin's arms flying up, her body falling in slow motion.

"Do not blame yourself. You cannot bargain with evil and hate. Until now they attack government patrols and raid villages at will."

"Until now? Don't they still own the countryside?"

"People are resisting. Joining New SUN and fighting back."

"New SUN?"

"You do not know of the New SUN Resistance?"

Reya remembered that Mai-Lin had mentioned people who'd escaped to some mountains. But she had assumed that was a myth—something to give the captive women false hope. But if the place was real, it might be a possible sanctuary for herself. "Is this resistance group in some mountains?"

"Yes, the Blue Mountains, northeast of here. That is New SUN's base. Most people there are blenders and villagers who have experienced 'gade attacks. The New SUN colony has become a small city with hundreds of people, perhaps a thousand by now. All are willing to fight for the society of tolerance that SUN intended. Regardless of Alliance indifference, we will see the Blending Program succeed."

Reya watched lantern shadows flutter across Bettina's face. "You said 'we.'"

"Yes, I am part of New SUN."

"Then, why are you here in the middle of the forest?"

"I am a forward scout. These villagers have been kind to me, but they are in danger as long as I am here. I will soon return to the Blue Mountains with my report of 'gade activities in this sector. After you rest, I must question you about the 'gades you encountered."

Reya nodded. "I have plenty to tell you about the bastards." She recalled the blinding flash of the explosion. Hugging Mai-Lin against the rough tree bark as debris smashed through the forest. She looked at Bettina. "What did you do with Mai-Lin?"

"We buried her in the village graveyard. The headwoman wrapped her in a new backcloth. It is their way of preparing her journey to the spirit world." Bettina paused. "How much did you know about Mai-Lin's activities?"

"Activities?"

"Your friend was from New SUN—possibly a scout like me."

"Mai-Lin? Couldn't be. Never said anything, and I was her closest friend."

"Scouts cannot reveal themselves. It would place friends in danger."

Reya lay back on the mat and eased her throbbing arm across her stomach. My God, she thought. Little Mai-Lin had been a gutsy scout? A spy? Reya wiped her eyes as she thought of her. Of her face and trusting friendship. Reya turned her head toward Bettina. "How do you know Mai-Lin worked for this 'New SUN'?"

Bettina opened her hand to reveal a twine necklace with a small wooden elephant painted forest-green. "This is New SUN's symbol. Neither the spirit of the elephant nor New SUN can be stopped."

Reya fingered the crudely carved elephant and searched Bettina's eyes. "I never saw Mai-Lin wear this."

"It was hidden in her shoe. It would be a death sentence to wear the elephant in a 'gade camp. Your friend had courage to even possess this."

"May I have it? I have nothing of hers."

Bettina closed her fist. "You cannot wear it. Only those who join New SUN—and are willing to die for it—carry the elephant. You must keep it hidden from sight." She slowly unfolded her hand and held out the necklace. "Do you have a place to hide it?"

Reya clutched the necklace, sensing a tingle of Mai-Lin's spirit. "Yes, and I will treasure it."

TALKING CAR

Only hours after D'Shay and Nakhoza had arrived
in Nswibe, a little girl ran into the common house
where D'Shay and Nakhoza were talking over cornbread
and tea. They glanced up at the panting child.

"'Scuse me, Miss SUN Lady, but—"

"Please—call me Nakhoza. Except for this uniform,
I'm a Chewan girl, like you."

The girl nodded, her eyes wide. "Miss Nakhoza, your
car . . . it is talking. I think maybe they be car spirits."

"Thank you, child." She smiled. "But don't worry, I
can shoo away car spirits. They are not evil."

D'Shay followed Nakhoza outside. "I'm coming along in case the car spirits get nasty."

She chuckled as they jogged to the Rover hidden in brush at the village edge. Nakhoza leaned in the window to listen.

The receiver crackled with static. "Repeating orders... SUN-304, report immediately. SUN-304, acknowledge transmission."

She glanced at D'Shay and put her fingers to her lips. D'Shay nodded, then leaned against the still-warm metal of the Rover. Nakhoza threw the "Transmit" switch. "SUN-304, here. I'm patrolling for 'gade activity north of the city, over."

"Your current mission has been cancelled, 304. Your new orders are to report back to headquarters immediately."

She glanced at D'Shay, her eyes flashing with anger.

D'Shay started to say, "What's the—" but Nakhoza clapped her hand over his mouth.

"304, did you copy? I repeat, did you copy?"

She tapped her fingers on the car door, then said, "Headquarters, headquarters. Heavy static. Cannot copy. Please repeat." The dispatcher repeated the message. She waited a moment. "I've lost you, headquarters. I will try to re-contact tomorrow. SUN-304 signing off."

Nakhoza flipped off the receiver then leaned against the Rover.

"So, they're recalling you?" asked D'Shay.

She waved him quiet. "Give me a moment. I am too angry." She turned and kicked at the car door.

D'Shay stepped back as she continued to kick and shout something, maybe Chewan curses.

She turned back, shooting a glance at D'Shay. "Please excuse my outburst."

"Hey, it's okay," said D'Shay.

"They are recalling me and will demote me to a GlobeTran guard to police alley gangs in the city. That's what happened to most of my SUN colleagues."

"You can't go up against those alley thugs, Nakhoza. They like to cut up cops and blenders. Can't you fight the recall? Go over their heads and talk to a Global Alliance officer?"

She shook her head. "The Alliance has contracted their offices and command centers to GlobeTran. SUN personnel are being phased out. And GlobeTran might be glad to see a SUN field officer go missing in an alley. There would be one less person on their payroll and they'd be rid of another troublesome believer in the ideals of SUN. I wonder if the GlobeTran leaders have their own agenda here in Africa."

"Why would they?" asked D'Shay. "They're just contractors for the Alliance."

"Yes, but there is much opportunity for corruption with the power the Alliance gave to GlobeTran."

"Maybe you—we—should stay here ... until you figure out where to go."

She smiled. "I already know where I am going." She

reached in her shirt and dangled a delicately carved green elephant at the end of a string. "They may try to eliminate the SUN program, but it is already arising in a new form." She nodded to the northeast. "I intend to join the New SUN movement in the Blue Mountains. Despite 'gades and the takeover by GlobeTran, the ideals of SUN will live on."

D'Shay saw the shine in her eyes as she looked to the northeast. Damn, he thought, he'd never met anyone like this girl. Never met anyone with a burning dream like hers. He'd always just drifted with fate. If he could only sense some of the purpose and the arrowlike focus of Nakhoza's.

She smiled at him, and—Whoa!—it was like a sucker punch in the gut. What was that about? No girl had ever made that happen.

"Shall we ask Lingana about staying in the village?"

It took a moment for her words to register. Finally D'Shay said, "Uh ... sure, sure. Ask Lingana."

SPIRIT HOME

"The Goblin said: 'There used to be people / there used to be people here / here in the Chief's village / it is overgrown like the veld / there used to be people.'"

—*Lamba proverb*

A week passed. Nakhoza had been given a cot in Lingana's house. After being invited to stay as long as she needed, she volunteered to fortify the vulnerable village with booby traps and trip-wires—skills she learned in SUN training to combat 'gade incursions.

At the same time, Giambo grudgingly allowed D'Shay to cram into a corner near Jaym's sleeping mat. "But you gonna work for room and food," said Giambo. "Gonna work in quarry like a man."

"Let's talk about that," said D'Shay. "Look—you've got Jaym. I'd just get in the way in your quarry. Probably accidentally poke one of you with a pick. I've got other skills you and the village could use."

"Only skill I see is you looking at pretty girls and being a lazy NorthAm."

D'Shay shook his head, feigning a look of disappointment. "You've misjudged me, my friend. I'm a master carpenter. I can build anything."

"How that be good for me?" Giambo waved at his hut. "I have house with good roof. Only little rain leak in."

"Yeah, but I can fix it so *no* rain leaks in. And I can even build an addition to your ... home. I can double its size. You'd have extra room and privacy from Jaym and me. And when we move out, you'll have a mansion all to yourself." D'Shay tried to keep a convincing smile, wondering if he could tackle a project of this scale.

Giambo rubbed his chin stubble, eyes narrowed in thought. "You build inside toilet for me too."

"Sorry, I'm a carpenter, not a plumber."

"No toilet, no deal."

"Your outhouse looks okay to me."

"It be hot and smell bad."

"I can fix up your privy. I'll put vents and screens at the top. I can even add a latch to the door and give it a paint job—your choice of color."

Giambo nodded slowly. "But where you get boards to make my house bigger? There be no extra in Nswibe."

D'Shay grinned and pointed toward the Nswibe's ghost village. "I can get all the lumber I need from those useless houses over there."

Giambo paled, his eyes wide.

———

That evening D'Shay walked with Jaym and Nakhoza. They stopped short of Old Nswibe with its tattered curtains in vacant windows.

"Look," said D'Shay with a sweep of his arm. "All that lumber is going to waste. Damn, you should have seen Giambo when I told him my idea."

"You're talking about messing with Nswibe ghosts," said Jaym. "They think the old town is full of spirits. Very taboo stuff."

"There's gotta be a way," said D'Shay. "Giambo's bedbugs are gonna suck me dry. Might as well sleep on an ant mound."

"We had much the same in my old village," said Nakhoza. "We needed lumber for new houses, but the elders would not allow us to go near the Death Homes. But after much debate my people came up with a solution. Maybe it will work here too."

———

D'Shay arranged a meeting with Mr. Zingali the next day. "Sir, we need lumber from just one of the old houses," he said.

Mr. Zingali leaned back in his chair and sucked his pipe. "You wanna bring much bad luck to our people? Spirits very strong. Ruin crops, make peoples sick."

"Nakhoza knows how we can satisfy the spirits of a ghost house."

Mr. Zingali shook his head behind a curl of smoke. "Spirit need house."

"Yeah, but the same house?"

———————

Two days later D'Shay, Mr. Zingali, and the village shaman solemnly approached the old village. The shaman carried a painted staff carved with faces and figures. The end of the staff was plumed with sunbird feathers. He chanted and brushed the ghost house with the feathers. Mr. Zingali stood back, his face drawn and anxious. D'Shay stood behind, cradling the miniature house he had created from scraps of plywood and tin. He had even painted it in colors the shaman said would appease ghosts—mostly reds and blacks. At the shaman's insistence, D'Shay added a little chair, table, and bed.

After twenty minutes of feathering and chanting, the shaman cautiously listened to the breeze whispering through curtains in a window frame. The man had his eyes squeezed shut, then chanted into the house as he tightly gripped his staff. Finally he nodded and backed away.

"This house spirit agree. Will trade new house for old, and blood of one fine chicken." He nodded to D'Shay who lay the miniature house by the front door. Mr. Zingali held the chicken by its feet. The shaman took it and slashed its throat. He spattered blood from the flapping hen, making a red trail from the ghost home to the tiny house.

The shaman looked exhausted. "It is done. The spirit

will move tonight." He nodded toward D'Shay. "In morning you take house wood you need—but only this one house. And you must not touch new spirit house," he said, looking at the tiny red and black surrogate. "Must not touch it forever."

———————

Several days later D'Shay stood at the top of a shaky ladder pounding nails into a ceiling joist of Giambo's addition. Without a proper level the walls were a little wavy, but solid enough. Besides, Giambo didn't seem to notice during his daily inspections.

"Hey, DuShay!" shouted Nakhoza from below.

"Damn, girl! Glad to see you, but don't sneak up like that. I about jumped off the ladder."

"Sorry, Mr. Carpenter Man," she grinned. "You be ready for tea break with me and Lingana?"

He climbed down and unbuckled his makeshift carpenter's belt. "Always ready for a break with a pretty lady. Even if it's for tea."

She laughed. "Still don't like Chewan tea? I think it be very good for you health—specially you column."

"My column? My column is doing fine, thank you very much. It's just that I miss coffee. Only good thing about the Corridor was that you could get black-market coffee. It was like gold, but worth it when you could get it."

They walked to the communal table outside the meetinghouse where Lingana waited for them. She gave them both a bright smile. "How are you doing, Nakhoza? Are the village people treating you well?"

"I'm doing very well, thank you. And everyone has been very kind." She smiled at Lingana and sipped her tea. "I am so grateful to you and your parents for letting me stay." She nodded toward the hills. "It is so beautiful here."

Down the table Mrs. Zingali and her group of women friends eyed the trio. "Is your mother ever going to stop watching us?" whispered D'Shay.

Lingana stifled a laugh. "Mother has the eyes of a falcon and protects me like a lioness protects her cub. She distrusts outsiders, but I think she is a little better than when you first came, yes? At least we 'llowed to talk like this."

"But I still do not understand why Jay-em cannot join us," said Nakhoza. "You two be a couple, yes?"

Lingana's face flushed. "Mother and I thought he would leave…because I told him he is a danger to the village. But since you both come and stay, I think it is right that Jay-em be here also."

"Have you told your mama you like him?" asked Nakhoza.

"I do not tell her, but I think she knows. But still, Mother still does not trust mzungu boys. She 'specially be lioness about Jay-em 'cause he is white."

"But can't she see that Jaym's a great guy?" asked D'Shay. "He's even proven himself in the quarry. His work is bringing money in to the family. What's he have to do?"

Nakhoza glanced down the table. The older women

were gathering their cups, preparing to go back to their chores. "I will return in a few minutes. I need to talk with your mother."

Lingana reached for her arm. "Nakhoza, no! You will make things..."

But Nakhoza marched toward Mrs. Zingali. The older woman stiffened her back and crossed her arms at the approaching girl. D'Shay and Lingana watched silently as Nakhoza bowed slightly. The other women—their mouths tight and brows raised—left the two alone at the table.

"Mother will devour her," whispered Lingana.

"Don't be too sure," said D'Shay. "Nakhoza is no pussy-cat."

Lingana smiled. "You like Nakhoza, yes?"

D'Shay nodded. "Yeah, I do." He looked over to watch them talk. After several minutes he said, "Your mama doesn't look too happy with Nakhoza."

"But Mother's arms not crossed now, and she hasn't shouted."

Finally Nakhoza stood and gave the older woman a peck on the cheek. "Good God," said D'Shay. "She kissed your mama."

"That is a formal Chewan gesture. Mother would be insulted otherwise."

Nakhoza returned to Lingana and D'Shay with a quiet smile on her face.

"What happened?" asked Lingana, touching Nakhoza's hand.

"Oh, I just asked her if she ever wanted grandchildren."

Lingana blushed and fumbled her teacup.

"She wouldn't talk at first. She knew she was in a trap. She said a very soft, 'yes.'" Nakhoza sipped her cool tea. "But there be more."

"More?" said Lingana.

"I ask for little more freedom for Jay-em so he can help DuShay finish Giambo's house soon. She finally said 'okay.'"

Nakhoza gave D'Shay a quick wink, and—pow! The fist into his gut again. Those magic eyes of hers ... But maybe she'd flirt like this with any guy. Better not make a fool of himself. Can't show that cupid just knocked him senseless—again. He just smiled. "Bless you, Nakhoza. Getting those roof beams up on my own is a killer."

"So," continued Nakhoza, "starting tomorrow Jay-em will be working half days with you to finish."

D'Shay raised his eyebrows. "You're a miracle worker!"

With a straight face she said, "Did you expect less?" Then she laughed.

Damn, she was something, thought D'Shay. She had such class and brains, and here he was, just a guy from a bad-ass NorthAm hood who drifted through school. Hoping for her was like wanting to possess a brilliant sunrise.

"Did Mother say anything ... else?" asked Lingana.

Nakhoza fingered her chin as if to remember. "Oh, yes. Your sweet mother agrees that it is proper for you and Jay-em to spend one hour each day to visit—with supervision of course. She says she wants you to report in a week if Jay-em seems a good 'nough man for her grandbabies."

Lingana looked at her cup and wiped her mouth to hide the hint of a smile.

Nakhoza stood and stretched. "I must get back to my work."

"How's it going out there?" asked D'Shay.

"Goes well. When I began SUN patrol work, I did not think I would ever get to use my counterinsurgency training. The villagers have learned very quickly. We now have several strong defensive teams." She helped Lingana stack the cups and spoons on a wicker tray. "We will be done in a day or two, then I'll give you a tour of the defenses. I think you will be impressed."

How could I be more impressed? thought D'Shay. But he just said, "You'll probably have to give everyone in the village a tour, right?"

"Yes. They must know the locations of the mines and traps." She paused, looking at the tidy homes and children running and laughing in the square. "I have seen the ruins of unprepared villages. I will not let that happen to Nswibe."

HEALING

Wounds and cuts: African mallow is often
used as a poultice for healing wounds and skin
inflammations. The powdered flowers and leaves
have been shown to stimulate cellular regeneration,
cleansing, and detoxification.

—*African Herbal Medicine by S. Ptunda*
(Bundwa Press, 2065)

Reya lay in leaf-filtered sunlight on the small patio.
She left her recovering bullet wound exposed to the
healing of sunshine and cool morning air. It had been a
week now, and the inflammation had finally begun to
recede. She propped herself up to watch rainbow-painted
butterflies drift through the flowers of the small garden,
and to see bright sunbirds swooping through the forest
canopy. This highland forest village was an oasis of beauty
and peace, but she knew it could turn into a hell if the
'gades discovered it.

She wondered how far she had staggered through the
forest carrying Mai-Lin. Was she now far enough in that
'gades wouldn't find her?

Mai-Lin. Each morning Reya laid fresh flowers on Mai-Lin's small grave in the village cemetery. When she did, she knelt and cried, placing her hand on the warm earth and whispering to Mai-Lin: "You were almost free of them. You were so brave and strong. I want you back, Mai-Lin. We should be traveling together. It's so unfair that those bastards…"

Bettina stepped from the small house and said, "Good morning, Reya."

Reya smiled. *Thank God for Bettina.*

"It's time to change your bandage." She knelt beside Reya's cot and carefully checked the wound. "It is healing well, Reya. No maggots, and most of the pus has drained. You will need to learn how to use the muscles in that arm again because some of the tissue has been destroyed."

"I'm so glad you are here," said Reya.

Bettina's expression grew more serious as she wrapped the gauze. "Reya, I must leave in a few days. But do not worry, the village women will continue to look after you."

Reya's eyes widened. For a moment she couldn't breathe. "No. Please, Bettina. Don't leave me here. Please!"

Bettina took Reya's shaking hand. "I must return to New SUN and report on activities in this area. The 'gades have infiltrated these highlands to a much greater extent than we realized. We will need to liberate these highlands by taking out one 'gade camp at a time. You and the other women fought like New SUN warriors, but our people need to continue what you and Mai-Lin began."

Reya nodded, but kept a firm grip on Bettina's hand. "When will you leave?"

"In three days."

Reya said nothing for a moment, but her expression changed from fright to determination. "I'm going with you."

"No, that's impossible. It is a journey of seventy kilometers. You must rest here and heal."

"I have healed enough. I'm strong and will make it."

"But Reya, you must not—"

"No, Bettina. I must...and I will."

'GADES

"A person does not begin to forge a gun when the war has already arrived in the village."

—Njanja proverb, East Africa

After supper Jaym watched Lingana's slim figure move gracefully beneath the jug of water balanced on her head. She turned slightly and gave him a soft smile. He felt a rush in his chest of… something. Was it just adrenaline because a pretty girl smiled at him?

The sun was dropping behind the tree line and the clouds started to catch fire. He headed back to the "D–J House"—that was what D'Shay had christened the Giambo addition.

On the way he watched a flock of parrots swoop in elegant formation against the sunset as they sought their roost for the night. He stretched and rubbed out the aches in his shoulders. It had been a month now, and he actually enjoyed the morning quarry work and his afternoon carpentry with D'Shay. But what he ached for most was his daily hour with Lingana. Whenever Mrs. Zingali—their ever-present chaperone—dozed off during their hour together, he and Lingana held hands. Once, during a prolonged doze by her mother, she stole to his side of the table and let him put his hand on her warm, smooth thigh.

Even if he did have to leave someday, he was going to enjoy all these moments. Life had never been so sweet. Giambo had softened toward him these past weeks and gave him brotherly advice, such as, "Do not tell Lingana she not have nough fat on body." Jaym had tried not to smile. He loved her slim body—that tiny waist, the soft flair of her hips, those perfect legs. Another Giambo warning was, "Try not to complain 'bout her cooking. That make her much, much angry. She not good in kitchen. Never use 'nough spice."

Thank God, he thought. Chewan cuisine had pretty much seared off his taste buds as it was.

Jaym had nearly reached the house when a sudden clatter of cowbells from the woods made the parrots screech as they burst from their roosts.

Jaym froze, his stomach tight.

Voices. Shouting from the woods. Oh God. It's finally happening.

Someone rang the village bell. Villagers poured from their homes and Jaym ran with them to the square.

"Stay calm!" shouted Nakhoza. "Go to your assigned places. Hide as we have trained. Do nothing until you see them." A mother tried to calm a wailing baby. "Get children inside. Lanterns out. Now, go go go!"

Jaym craned his neck, trying to spot Lingana among the scrambling villagers.

"Come on, Jaymo," said D'Shay, tugging at his arm. "Get a move on. Lingana will be okay."

Jaym jogged with two dozen others toward the maize shed where a man and woman were already passing out weapons. They were antiques, but Nakhoza had drilled and drilled the villagers to make the most of what they had. Some were handed the spears of their grandfathers. Others got pitchforks, axes, or machetes. Jaym and D'Shay had had Corridor sim-training with rifles, so they and eight others were given the old Bulgarian single-shot rifles. Each rifleman was handed five precious bullets.

God, thought Jaym. Would the gunpowder still be good after a hundred years? No one had fired a single bullet in practice. Had to save every shot for this. If they were duds, all he'd have was a rifle-club.

An explosion and scream. A 'gade had hit one of Nakhoza's trip wires.

He and D'Shay scrambled to their rooftop positions. Giambo gripped his quarry pick and he limped toward the woods.

Another explosion. Screamed curses, then random bursts of gunfire.

Jaym ducked at the whiz of bullets zipping overhead. One thwacked into the next house. He kept flat against the roof, waiting—looking down his sights for silhouettes to emerge from the woods.

Now a warrior's cry from one of the villagers. The 'gades had reached the first lines of defense—the volunteers who preferred spears and machetes. Giambo would be with them, swinging his pick.

More shouting and machine-gun chatter. A scream pierced the sounds of fighting. Jaym's arms prickled with goosebumps. Oh God, was the scream from Giambo or one of the other villagers?

Another mine exploded, lighting the trees in a brief flash. Jaym still saw no sign of approaching 'gades. Had the front line of villagers held them off? No, impossible. Not against automatic weapons.

"Do not fire!" shouted Nakhoza. "Not until you cannot miss."

Jaym couldn't see her in this light, but knew she'd be at the village edge, braced against the wall of a house, both hands steadying her pistol.

One of the mines had set a tree on fire. It now burned like a torch to light the scene of fighting. Jaym got up on one knee to look for silhouettes of 'gades. He saw no movement except for the dancing of shadows cast by the flaming tree.

It was silent now. If the 'gades had taken out the villagers, were they now flanking the village to storm in from the rear? He tried to slow his rapid breathing.

There! Shadows moving from the woods. He raised his rifle and sighted in the nearest figure.

The man shouted in Chewan. Giambo!

Whistles and warrior cries erupted in the village. Jaym lay his face against the warm roof and whispered, "Thank God."

"Jaymster!" shouted D'Shay. "The front line whupped them. We're home free!" D'Shay slid from his rooftop and yelled, "Nakhoza! Where are you, oh gallant defender of Nswibe?"

Jaym heard her laugh. Lanterns flared and villagers embraced. He slid from his rooftop position and joined the cheering, dancing crowd below. "Not yet!" shouted Nakhoza. "Any dead or wounded?"

"Only seven dead 'gade peoples," bellowed Giambo. He strutted to the village edge and wiped his pick on the grass.

"Jay-em," said Lingana behind him. She looked down. "I was ... afraid for you."

He leaned his rifle against a house and held her tightly. She shivered in his arms. He squeezed her and looked toward the sinister silhouette of the woods. Smoke from one of the exploded mines slithered as a ghostly ground fog. He turned away and stroked Lingana's back.

Nakhoza tapped Jaym and Lingana on their shoulders. "Please, get D'Shay and Giambo. We all need to talk."

When they were gathered, the lantern light showed her face tight with anger. "These 'gades did not find Nswibe by chance," she said.

"Then, how?" asked Jaym. "The village is way off the grid."

"Who knows you were assigned here, Jaym?" she asked.

"The Alliance and SUN."

"Oh, crap," muttered D'Shay. "And GlobeTran, right? That's why they wanted you SUN people recalled."

"Exactly," said Nakhoza. "Someone in GlobeTran is informing 'gades of blender assignments. They must want the Blender Program to fail."

"But why?" asked Lingana. "Is not GlobeTran here to protect us? It is the arm of the Alliance. It is supposed to assist in the SUN mission. Yes?"

"GlobeTran is a corporation. Think of the power it would have if it joined forces with 'gades. They would control Africa."

"The Global Alliance would stop them," said Jaym.

"Perhaps," said Nakhoza. "But the Alliance has entrusted their firepower and troops to GlobeTran. And the Alliance may not be aware of what is happening here. When they find out it may be too late."

"Then 'gades will attack us again," said Giambo.

"Yes," said Nakhoza. "They will."

———

The next morning Jaym and D'Shay volunteered to help bury the 'gades. Some had been killed with machetes or spears, but the two who hit A.P. mines were only scattered body parts. While walking through grass, Jaym stumbled over a leg, its boot still in place. He swallowed back his breakfast. He toed the leg toward the grave, then kept shoveling.

Giambo wandered over to Jaym and pointed to three

bodies swarming with flies. Two were white, the other African. All wore black tee shirts and stocking caps. "I kill three for my Nyanko. But more will die for her." He spat at the bodies, then limped back to the village.

While Jaym and others dug, he saw Nakhoza and her team working nearby to reset the trip wires, fill exploded mine craters, and camouflage their work with leaves and branches.

Jaym and D'Shay used their shovels to roll a body into the finished pit. Others flipped in body parts with shovels. Sweat ran off Jaym's back as he shoveled dirt over the gore as fast as he could. Finally they packed down the earth, then dragged vines, twigs, and leaves over the mass grave. The final touch was randomly placing lichen-covered rocks over the area to make the site blend with the rocky field.

Jaym and D'Shay tossed their tee shirts over their shoulders and picked up their shovels. "I need a big cold jug of Nswibe brew," said D'Shay as they dragged their shovels back to the village.

"I'll join you," said Jaym. "But you know it's not gonna be cold."

"I can dream, can't I? Cold, with just a slight head of foam. Pure amber to cleanse the soul."

They walked in silence for a few meters. "The 'gades will be after Reya too, won't they?" asked Jaym.

D'Shay nodded. "Yeah. Our Plan-B has kinda gone to hell. No way to warn her."

"Maybe she'll get wind of what's going on and get to another village."

D'Shay nodded. "If anybody's gonna make it, it'll be Reya."

They propped their shovels against the toolshed and, with the other diggers, washed in a communal trough. Women poured in buckets of clean water as silty water ran out the other end.

Jaym splashed water through his hair, letting it run down his chest and back.

D'Shay was quiet for a moment, his face sober as he wiped water from his eyes.

"What's the matter?" asked Jaym.

"Something Nakhoza told me." He wiped wet hands on his shorts. "She figures we're gonna get hit again, maybe soon. Says 'gades usually sweep an area with more than one team."

Lingana poured her bucket of water in the trough and smiled at Jaym. "What are you boys talking about?"

D'Shay and Jaym glanced at each other. "Um, the raid last night," said Jaym.

Lingana nodded, waiting.

"Have you talked to Nakhoza?" asked Jaym.

Her smile faded. "Yes. She told me she listened to the com in her Rover this morning. Says there is much chatter 'bout 'gades, but no one is sure where they are."

"I know where seven of 'em are," said D'Shay. "Now if you two will excuse me, I'm going to consume some fine village brew." He pulled on his tee shirt and headed toward the communal hall.

Jaym and Lingana found some shade under a tree and

sat on the dry grass. "I worry," said Lingana. "Nakhoza can do only so much to help protect our village. We have brave men and women who will fight, but we also have many children and old people."

He took one of her hands in his and stroked her slender fingers. "Now we have the 'gade weapons," he said. "Seven automatic rifles and ten handguns. It won't be easy to take the village."

"But if they do…" She squeezed his hand. "I am frightened for my family."

He nodded. "I'm frightened for you. I don't know what I'd…"

Her large eyes searched his face. "Me too … Jay-em."

TAKING LEAVE

"Keep your eyes on your destination, not where you stumbled."

—*Yoruba proverb, Nigeria*

Thanks to medicinal herbs and sunshine, Reya's thorn gashes had sealed and were now merely red welts. The wound in her bicep still oozed, but the pain was bearable. But she wondered if she was really strong enough for a three- or four-day trek with Bettina through forest and hilly trails. She had to be. If not, she'd die trying.

This was departure day. She and Bettina had fashioned a backpack of sorts from a baby-toting backcloth provided by one of the village women. She would pack two liters of water, a kilo of cornmeal, a pouch of groundnuts, and a baby-food jar filled with brown goo to rub into her wound each day.

Bettina stepped outside the house. "We will leave near dusk and travel all night. Perhaps you should get some rest, Reya."

Reya smiled up at her. "I'm fine. Besides, I'm too pumped up to sleep."

"What are you making?"

"A new sling. My old one is okay for lounging, but I need something more stable for hiking."

"Yes, you could reopen the wound." She took the scissors from Reya. "You need two hands for this heavy material." As Bettina cut the cloth she said, "You realize, Reya, I will do all I can to help you reach the Blue Mountains, but if..."

"Yes, I know. I'm willing to take that chance. But I can make it. Even if you do have to leave me behind, I will still get there. Maybe days or weeks later, but nothing's going to stop me."

Bettina nodded, her face somber. "Here let's try on your new sling."

Reya grimaced as Bettina removed the old cloth and tied her wounded arm securely with the new sling. Bettina stepped back and grinned. "Oh, very fashionable. The people at New SUN will be so jealous."

Reya laughed. "Yes, everyone there will also want an orange and green paisley sling."

Bettina stood. "Can I get you anything before I go in?"

"No, but I've meant to ask you—do you have some way to contact Wananelu? I have a couple of blender friends and I want them to know—"

"No. I have a hand-com but only use one secure channel to the New SUN base. Sorry, but a message to Wananelu would allow 'gades to triangulate our position and movements."

Reya sighed, adjusted her new sling, and then lay back

in the shade as a slight breeze arose to help tame the blistering afternoon.

———————

That night Reya and Bettina ate their supper with the village women. There were hugs and farewells all around as the two girls donned their packs for the journey. Before they left, Reya laid a cluster of delicate pink lilies on Mai-Lin's grave, now covered with a velvet layer of new grass. She fingered the wooden elephant around her neck. Then, in the moonlit night, she followed Bettina to the trail near the village and into the forest.

OFF GUARD

"When an enemy digs a grave for you, God gives
you an emergency exit."

—*Kirundi proverb*

Six days now since the 'gade attack on Nswibe. Two guards were now posted each night, but so far there had been no sign of 'gades. Nakhoza monitored her police radio, but nothing was mentioned about the Nswibe region. Villagers relaxed and went back to their chores.

It was planting season, so women spent the days in the vast garden below the village. New plots of maize were laid out and seeded. Gourds and melons were planted in mounds, and irrigation ditches to the banana and guava trees were cleared. Bucket brigades of women passed well water down to flow in the ditches.

D'Shay was busy with a couple of other village carpenters rebuilding a termite-riddled wall on the communal house. Jaym was back in the quarry with Giambo. He was stronger than he'd ever been. His back, arm, and shoulder muscles had thickened, and the rhythm of the picks swinging at the rock was like a mantra. Sometimes Giambo would loosen up enough to sing work songs in time with their strokes. Jaym had no clue what the words were, but he enjoyed Giambo's deep chant and he caught the flow, sometimes trying a verse or two.

While he swung his pick, he thought about the times he and Lingana had found brief moments alone. Times when he felt the warmth of her slim body against his, the sweet scent of her hair—something like lavender. He pictured her now, washing in the morning, rubbing a damp cloth up her chocolate-smooth arms and down her slim belly and legs. Then she'd splash a little lavender water in her hands and stroke it through her hair. For him.

Footsteps pattered down the trail. It was Lingana's youngest sister. Jaym was about to swing his pick when he saw the terrified look on the girl's face. Oh God, not again. Please, not now.

She spoke breathlessly to Giambo, pointing beyond the quarry.

"Are they coming?" asked Jaym.

"Not yet." Giambo walked across the quarry to peer across the valley. He pointed to brown smoke drifting through the valley mist. "There. 'Gades make attack on Mayukoana village."

Jaym shuddered. "That's only five or six klicks away."

Giambo nodded. "We must prepare."

They hurried back to the village where men had already gathered, arguing and gesturing in different directions. Many shouted, shaking spears and guns. Village women, their faces anxious, clustered behind with the children.

Lingana ran to Jaym and Giambo.

"What're the men arguing about?" asked Jaym.

"Some do not listen to Nakhoza. They want to catch the 'gades at Mayukoana Village. Try to ambush them." She hugged herself, her face tight. "But others agree with Nakhoza and say we must prepare for attack here. Stand our ground. There may be many 'gades this time. We cannot know."

Nakhoza stepped forward. "Men. Please listen. We must—"

A wild-eyed man stepped in front of her, made a war cry and shook his spear. Giambo stepped forward and snatched the man's spear. "*That be 'nough!*" he roared. "Listen to Nakhoza. Did she not show us how to stop 'gades before? *Yes!* You all be brave warriors, but we must not fight between us. Nakhoza girl know much 'bout fighting 'gades. *So hear her words!*"

Lingana's father stepped forward. "Giambo be right. Listen to SUN girl. We must fight together, or 'gades win. Then 'gades take you womans and children. That be what you warriors want?"

The man who pushed Nakhoza aside pointed at Jaym and D'Shay, snarling in Chewan.

"Speak English!" snapped Giambo. "Be man 'nough so mzungu boys hear your words."

"Give blender boys to 'gades," shouted the man. "Give them what they want and we be safe."

Giambo's eyes flashed as he scanned the faces of the

men. "We not gonna kiss 'gade feet. Cannot bargain with 'gades. Even if we give blender boys, they still punish village bad. Take womans, burn Nswibe. Only choice be to fight."

Men glanced at one another. Most nodded, then looked to Nakhoza.

She stepped forward and raised her voice, her chin high. "Men and women of Nswibe, assemble into your teams. Prepare to defend your village and families, A Team," she said to a squad of five women. "Are mines set and camouflaged?"

"Yes," replied a short, muscular woman. "We also add more trip wires."

"Good. These 'gades may not know of the fate of last week's raid. So they probably take the same path through our woods to attack. But there might be more of them this time. We cannot know. Is Team B ready?" A half-dozen men and women nodded. A woman hefted one of the 'gade automatic rifles.

"You can use that?" asked Nakhoza.

"I practice good and mem'rize levers," said the woman. "I shoot only two bullets in practice, but hit bottle at twenty meters with second bullet. I save rest for 'gades."

Nakhoza nodded and pointed to the trail. "Your team has the most firepower, so cover the trail. Other teams take same positions as—"

Bursts of gunfire.

Bullets spattered dust in the square.

Jaym grabbed Lingana by the wrist and pulled her behind a wall. He heard the sickening thud of lead hitting flesh as people tried to scramble away. A half-dozen villagers in the square were cut down in seconds. The shots came from upslope, behind the village.

"Stay in your teams!" shouted Nakhoza.

Jaym couldn't see her, but she must have reached cover. But where was D'Shay? With Nakhoza?

Nakhoza shouted over the sounds of gunfire. "Team B, save ammunition! Wait until they reach the firing point. If they make it past the perimeter, Team C, fight for your village!"

Team C, thought Jaym. The guys with spears and machetes. Giambo would be with them with his pick. They would fight to the last. They all knew these 'gades wouldn't be taking prisoners.

More bullets tore through the village, spat dirt across dead and wounded in the square, and ripped into homes.

Jaym saw Nakhoza's silhouette move from behind a wall. She raised her rifle and shouted, "You are warriors! Make your—"

Nakhoza spun, then crumpled to the dirt. "Nakhoza's hit!" shouted Jaym. "Somebody get to Nakhoza!"

A figure darted out. Had to be D'Shay, thought Jaym. Bullets pinged as D'Shay dragged Nakhoza's form from the open. "Come on D'Shay," whispered Jaym. "Don't get hit."

Lingana lunged. "I must help her."

Jaym grabbed her by the arm. "No, Lingana! You'd never make it across the square!"

She tried to jerk free. "Let me go! I can run fast. They will not—"

"Lingana! I . . . won't let you die."

She eased back, her eyes confused, her chin quivering. He pulled her tight against him. "We have to make it."

More gunfire. Wounded crying for help. A child wailing.

Jaym glanced at the fallen villagers in the square. One man's arm lay across an automatic rifle. Jaym clamped his jaw. Could he retrieve it? He had to. All he carried was a 'gade pistol and two clips of ammo. He glanced from behind the wall. Three 'gades rushed downhill from the brush. They spread out, running in a crouch. They weren't firing now, but swept their weapons back and forth as they looked for targets.

Jaym spotted a villager behind a log, his rifle barrel blackened and leveled at the approaching 'gades. The man held his fire just as Nakhoza had drilled all of them. *Don't waste your ammo on the first 'gades*, she had said. *Not until they were thirty meters from the first houses. When they reached that point, open up.*

"Lingana," whispered Jaym. "I have to get a rifle. I'll make a run into the square when our people open fire." He pulled the pistol from his belt. "Here, take this. It's got a full clip. Here's another clip. Remember to hold it with both hands when you fire."

She wiped her eye and nodded. "Don't be . . . killed, Jay-em."

"No way, I promise."

HAND TO HAND

"The fighter does not recklessly shoot away his arrows."

—*African proverb*

———————

Jaym peered around the corner of the house. The three forward 'gades were closing in. They had almost reached the thirty-meter "open fire" distance.

One of the 'gades waved his arm and the three dropped into prone positions. They opened fire, spraying the village at will.

Damn! Now a dozen other 'gades rushed from the forest. They were covered by blistering fire from the three prone in the grass.

A villager shouted and Nswibe guns opened up on the charging 'gades. When the villagers began to fire, the dozen charging 'gades dropped to safety in the grass, continuing to rake the homes.

The bullets of the defenders tore wildly across the field. Most ripped uselessly through grass and brush.

It was now or never. Jaym dashed past bodies in the square and grabbed the fallen rifle. He sprinted behind another house. He panted, clutching the gun against his chest. "Villagers! Hold your fire!" he shouted. He tried his rough Chewan. *"Chonde! Iai, iai!* Please, no. Don't shoot! They *want* you to waste your ammo. *Hold your fire till I give the signal!"*

Only sporadic shots now. Finally, nothing from the villagers. The dozen 'gades started to advance in a crouch as their forward scouts fired covering bursts.

Jaym looked across the square to see Lingana, her back to a wall, the pistol clutched with both hands as he had shown her. She stared at him, her eyes wide. If only D'Shay were here to cover him and watch out for Lingana. But he'd be with Nakhoza—unless she was dead. She couldn't be dead, or D'Shay would be out front, fighting like a wild man. He had to be with another squad covering the north side of the village.

Jaym scanned the other buildings. Men and women crouched behind their hiding places—house walls, maize silos, stacks of firewood.

At last, the dozen 'gades had crept to the thirty-meter mark. Jaym raised up and shouted. "Riflemen! Now! *OPEN FIRE!"* He steadied his automatic against the wall of the house. *Aim at their knees,* Nakhoza had drilled them. *The rifle will kick upward. You must shoot low in short bursts.*

The rifle butt shuddered against his shoulder. He fought to keep the muzzle down as bullets chattered and brass clattered at his feet. My God! Three 'gades were thrown backward into the grass. Had he...?

The villagers opened up. More 'gades fell, but the rest

screamed like animals and ran forward, firing from the hip. Bullets tore through the village, ripping into adobe and splintering wood walls.

Jaym leaned out and fired more bursts. Dust kicked. Another 'gade down.

Oh God. His rifle jammed! He crouched and jerked free the magazine. Shit! Out of ammo!

'Gades had breached the perimeter. It was house-to-house now. He sprinted back to Lingana. She clutched his waist as bullets whizzed like bees.

He took her pistol. "Stay here. Lie low against the wall. Pretend you're dead if they make it this far."

"Don't leave, Jay-em. You will die."

"That's not going to happen."

She put her palm against his chest, her wide eyes frightened.

He sensed the electric touch of her palm radiate through his body.

Jaym steadied the 9-mm in a two-handed grip, then stepped into the square and the deafening fire.

He froze. Two 'gades, not five meters away. A tattooed skinhead sprayed bursts of gunfire into homes. The other 'gade torched roofs.

Jaym raised his pistol, but a villager rushed from behind a hut with his pre-war rifle. The 'tooed 'gade turned and cut him down. He fired another burst into the body.

Jaym squeezed twice. The 'gade jerked. He turned, his sunglasses glinting. Jaym fired again. The 'gade's mouth opened and closed before he crumpled to the dirt.

The other 'gade hurled his torch.

Jaym ducked.

The 'gade grabbed his rifle.

Jaym steadied his pistol.

Click, click.

The 'gade laughed. "Always count your shots, boy." He raised his weapon.

Jaym fumbled the second clip. It fell to his feet.

"Go ahead," said the 'gade. "I'm a sport. Pick it up."

Jaym snatched up the clip.

"Tsk tsk. Too slow, hero."

A quick, dark movement behind the 'gade. The man jerked forward. The startled 'gade looked down at the curved steel point jutting from his chest. "Bloody ... hell," he gurgled. His gun fired wildly into the earth as he folded to the ground.

Giambo jerked his pick from the 'gade's back. He spat at the body and nodded to Jaym. "That be for Nyanko too."

Jaym nodded. "Thanks ... Giambo. You saved—"

"Not talk now. Still few 'gades to finish."

"Take the pistol," said Jaym. "I'll use the 'gades rifle."

He shook his head. "Pick better for me. Go that way," he pointed. "I go there. We finish this now." With his bloodstained pick against his chest he limped between houses, toward the sound of intense firing.

Jaym wove between burning houses, fallen villagers, and 'gades. He stopped. "Mr. Zingali!" The old man's eyes were glazed. He sat, propped against the wall, his hands clutched to his belly. Blood trickled between his fingers.

He nodded to a 'gade lying face up, an old spear run through his throat. "My grandfather spear still have power, yes?"

Oh God, thought Jaym. Lingana's father only had minutes to live. He wanted to shout for her, bring her to comfort her dying father. No, he couldn't. She'd be shot trying to get here. He wouldn't take that chance, even if it meant she'd hate him for letting her father die alone.

He took the older man's hand and nodded. "Yessir. Your grandfather's spear has great power. And so do you. But, please, let me get you to—"

"No, Jay-em. Be my time to die. It be good to die like warrior. Go to Lingana. Must save her."

"I will, but—"

"No. Leave me! Kill 'gades, protect Lingana—forever."

Jaym stepped back.

"Go!"

Jaym hesitated before saying, "Yessir, I understand."

He sprinted toward the shooting. Turning a corner he stopped. "D'Shay!"

"Jaymo. I knew they wouldn't get you." D'Shay held his rifle like a club. "Ran out of ammo."

"Is Nakhoza..."

D'Shay's face twisted. "Wounded, but alive. The women are taking care of her. How 'bout Lingana?"

"She's okay so far. Look, take the pistol. It's got a full clip. I think there are only a couple of 'gades left, but they're still shooting villagers. We can rush them together, maybe catch them off guard."

"Hey, smoke," said D'Shay. "They're torching the houses."

Staying in the shadows, Jaym and D'Shay trotted toward the flames now leaping above rooftops.

LOOK BEYOND

I have broken my nose on a stick,
I have broken my right hip,
I have something in my eye,
And yet I go on.

—*Somali poem*

R eya wasn't sure she could make it through that first
night of trekking through the woods, trying to keep
up with Bettina. Twice she stumbled and fell. She did
not scream when she hit the ground and the waves of red
nearly made her pass out.

She knew a scream might reveal them to 'gades. The
pain was nothing to the thought of being captured again.
Enslaved and raped again. When she fell, Bettina helped
her to her feet and held her steady as the red waves ebbed
and she could move once again.

At sunrise, they bedded dozens of meters from the
trail, hidden behind great stands of ferns and logs of fallen
trees. Reya was certain she couldn't sleep through the pain,
but within minutes she was out.

In the late afternoon, they awoke and made their meal of cornmeal mixed with canteen water. Bettina smiled and held up her tin cup. "*Salud.*"

"*Salud.*" Reya sipped the watery gruel. "Uck," she said. "This stuff is bad enough when it's cooked."

Bettina laughed. "It is good you can joke. I know you are in pain, but we have come almost to the edge of the forest. We came at least fifteen kilometers last night. I am amazed and pleased you could keep up."

"Nothing's going to stop me. And thank God you know the way out of here."

"Drink down your fine meal. We must be ready to go at dusk."

————

Again they walked through the night. Reya stumbled, but now she did not fall. Sweat soaked her back, and her arm throbbed with each footstep.

Sometime before dawn Bettina stopped. "We are coming to the edge of the forest, Reya. Come, only a few hundred meters and you will see something beautiful."

Reya hurried behind Bettina, her heart racing, a new hope rising in her chest.

At the forest edge the two girls looked across a wide valley with a serpentined stream glinting in moonlight. "Yes," said Reya, "the valley is beautiful, but…"

"No, Reya. Look beyond."

Beyond the valley floor rose a blanket of foothills. And beyond those, in misty haze—"Dear God. It's them. The Blue Mountains."

EXODUS

"Daylight follows a dark night."

—*Maasai proverb*

When the attack on Nswibe was over, the Nswibe survivors counted their dead. Seventeen men, women, and children from the village had died, a dozen more wounded. All thirteen 'gade attackers lay dead. Smoke hung low in the Nswibe valley and vultures were already circling.

D'Shay clutched Nakhoza's hand as Lingana knelt, probing Nakhoza's shoulder wound with a knife. Nakhoza grit her teeth as her body trembled with pain.

"I am sorry, Nakhoza," said Lingana softly. "But I must remove all the pieces of shirt in your wound."

"Thank God it wasn't a hollow point," said D'Shay.

Jaym watched Lingana, biting her lip, tweezering another bloody fragment of cloth from the bullet hole.

He scanned the bloodstained square. The dead men and women—including Mr. Zingali—were laid out in the common house. With its metal roof, it was one of the few untorched structures. Mrs. Zingali and other wives and husbands sat with their dead, praying aloud and chanting death songs to free their spirits.

Giambo limped over to Jaym. He wore a wad of blood-soaked gauze wrapped around the stump of his right ear. He didn't look at Jaym as he spoke. "You, Jay-em, and you, DuShay... fight like warriors today." He glanced at the bodies. "Nswibe pay big, big price to win the 'gades."

"Your father, Giambo... I'm—"

"He die a good death. A warrior's death. Mother frees his spirit now. What be important that Lingana be alive."

Lingana looked up at Giambo and gave him a sad smile. "And also you, my... brother."

"We kill many 'gades today, but we lose too many village people."

Nakhoza coughed. Her eyes teared as she grimaced in pain. "More 'gades will come," she said between clamped teeth. "That is... their way. They want to crush Chewena village by village."

"Your wound is clear now, Nakhoza." Lingana dropped the tweezers and last fragment of cloth in a metal pan. "I will now medicine and bandage it."

"I think we all must leave Nswibe immediately," said Nakhoza. "We cannot withstand another attack—we've lost too many. We must join the others."

"Those in the Blue Mountains?" asked Lingana.

Nakhoza nodded. "It is the place of renewal for the SUN movement. The New SUN people will create the rebirth of a new Africa. I want to be a part of that. You all should be a part."

"Don't talk, Nakhoza," said D'Shay.

She made a pained smile and nodded. She shut her eyes as Lingana salved and bandaged her wound.

Nswibe buried its dead. A day of digging, mourning, wailing, and tears. They dug the graves in the village garden. Seventeen whitewashed river stones marked the men, women, and children of the village. Each stone was inked with a name. Women lay offerings of flowers, toys, old spears.

After stripping the dead 'gades of weapons and ammunition, they tossed their bodies in a common grave.

The villagers took only food, water, goats, weapons, and the few small heirlooms they could carry—faded photographs, parts of a family shrine, and mementos of those who lay beneath the white stones.

They had more weapons now. Many with little ammo, but still enough firepower to get them past a couple of packs of 'gades. They discovered that the 'gades had shot up Nakhoza's Rover beyond use, so they set fire to it to be sure 'gades could salvage nothing.

Nakhoza and the other wounded were carefully placed in handcarts.

Jaym took Lingana's hand as they looked back at the smoking village. He touched a tear on her cheek. She looked up and gave him a shaky smile. "We will be all right, Jayem—yes?"

"Better than all right. Come on. Let's help start this new Africa."

Hand in hand they walked with the others on the dusty road to the west. Toward the hazy blue hills in the distance.

END

Acknowledgments

I'd like to thank the following people for making this book possible: agents Scott Treimel and John Cusick for pulling my work from the slush pile; Brian Farrey of Flux, who made it come to life; Ed Day at Llewellyn, who edited it; and to writer friends Anne Warren Smith and Linda Crew for critiquing very rough drafts. And a special thanks to Ken Fraundorf, my good writing buddy, who helped keep my spirits up during the very early stages.

About the Author

Michael Kinch is a freelance writer and the author of *Warts*, an educational book for middle graders. While working as a science librarian at Oregon State University, he taught a workshop in Malawi, Africa, and *The Blending Time*, his debut novel, arose from the experience. Visit him online at www.michaelkinch.com.